"Is there something else you wanted?" she asked, her heart kicking up shards of guilt.

He sat down in the chair across from her desk. "Yes. I want to stay here and avoid my sister's wedding and my parents' anniversary."

An impulse jumped into her mind. She needed to get to Vancouver. In less than a month, Dylan, and her one solid connection to the Matheson company, was going to be gone. It was the perfect opportunity, and before she could even think about it, she spoke. "I could go with you. Help you with your father's problem. Pose as your girlfriend. Could cover two things in one easy solution."

Dylan's head snapped up. He stared at her a moment, then nodded, a grin crawling along his lips. "You know, that would be a great idea. I think it could work just perfectly."

Lisa beat down a flurry of nerves.

Vancouver. Already.

Books by Carolyne Aarsen

Love Inspired

*Stealing Home

CAROLYNE AARSEN

lives in Alberta on a small ranch with her husband and the youngest of their four children. Carolyne's writing skills have been honed between being a stay-at-home mom, wife, foster mother, columnist and business partner with her husband in their logging operation and cattle ranch. Writing for Love Inspired has given her the wonderful opportunity to combine her love of the Lord with her love of a romantic story.

LOVE IS PATIENT

CAROLYNE AARSEN

Published by Steeple Hill Books™

STEEPLE HILL BOOKS

Steeple Hill®

ISBN 0-373-87258-5

LOVE IS PATIENT

How priceless is Your unfailing love. Both high and low find refuge in the shadow of Your wings.

—*Psalms* 36:7

This book is for all my readers,
young and old. Thanks for taking time to
let my stories into your lives. I'd also like to thank
Rik Hal for his sailing help. Hope I got it right.
Thanks also to Laurie Hanchard for helping me
with accounting information.

Chapter One

She hadn't thought he'd be this young. Or this tall.

And if Dylan Matheson knew the real reason she was applying for the job he advertised, Lisa Sterling suspected his gray-blue eyes could become as cold as arctic ice.

Lisa followed Dylan into his office. Another man stood as they entered. He looked older than Dylan and a little thicker around the middle.

"Lisa, this is Perry Hatcher. Perry, Lisa. He'll be sitting in on the interview, as well." Dylan performed the introduction as he strode around his large desk to his leather chair.

Lisa shook Perry's hand, feeling more comfortable with him than she had with her potential boss.

"Sit down, please," Dylan said, indicating the chair in front of the desk. The floor-to-ceiling windows behind him put him in shadow, giving her a tactical disadvantage.

He sat and hitched his chair forward in one smooth motion. Controlled and in charge. "So, Lisa Sterling. Tell me why you want to work for Matheson Telecom," Dylan said.

Lisa had memorized her spiel and practiced it in front of the mirror. It was positive. Confident.

But laying her reasons out in front of this very self-possessed man on his territory was a different proposition. She had expected an older man, not someone with thick brown hair that waved over his forehead, softening the harsh planes of his face.

Help me out here, Lord. I absolutely have to get this job. I promise…I'll go to church if I get it.

The prayer was automatic, and harkened back to when she and her stepbrother, Gabe, had their parents and they were a family that attended church regularly. The bargaining, however, was a new touch her stepfather would have disapproved of.

She overrode her second thoughts, took a deep breath and started.

"I know that you're a nationally known company that's expanding rapidly and that you have vision for the future direction of telecommunications." She kept her smile in place, held the cool gray-blue of his eyes and kept her hands held loosely in her lap to remind her to relax. "Your head office is in Vancouver, and was started by your father, and you started this branch office only a few years ago, but it's already growing." She glanced sidelong at Perry to include him in the conversation, but mostly to slow herself down.

Don't talk too much. Don't let Dylan Matheson

guess your information comes from inside. "This company is going places. I'd like to be a part of that."

But mostly I want to find out why your company fired my stepbrother after falsely accusing him of theft.

Wisely she kept the previous thought unvoiced.

Dylan Matheson nodded, apparently satisfied with her explanation. He handed Perry a copy of her résumé, then Dylan leaned back in his chair, his thumb stroking his chin as he read.

Lisa concentrated on slowing her racing heart, willing herself to be quiet.

When Matheson Telecom had first hired him, Gabe Haskell had spoken in glowing terms about the company and how pleased he was to get an accounting job with them right out of college. Lisa never had any hint that he was unhappy with his work or that they were unhappy with him.

This job was her best opportunity to find out what had really happened.

"When would you be free to begin?" Dylan asked, his voice quiet. Even. Controlled.

Lisa stifled the swift surge of hope. "I can start next week." She would need to give notice, but Tony knew she was looking for another job and he knew why.

"This job might require some travel," Dylan continued, folding his hands on the desk. "Would you be able to accompany me on business trips? Or is there a boyfriend who might object?"

"No boyfriend."

Though she had learned valuable lessons in the wrong kind of men from her mother's life, Lisa still managed to make her own mistakes in the boyfriend department.

Single life was less complicated, and practically heartbreak-free.

"Why do you want to leave your current job?" Dylan continued, glancing at her résumé. "Legal secretary at Mercurio, Donnelly and Abrams. Quite a reputable firm."

Lisa's heart flipped over.

This would be the trickiest part of the interview. She would have preferred not to use Tony as a reference. Explaining a gap of three years in a résumé, however, was harder than edging around the real reason she wanted to quit.

"I need a challenge and a change," she said, choosing her words with care. "I feel I've gone as far up professionally as I can reasonably hope."

And my married boss keeps coming on to me.

Dylan's gaze zeroed in on hers as if questioning her reply, but she didn't look away. Tony was the one at fault, not her.

"I was wondering if I might ask a few questions myself, Mr. Matheson, Mr. Hatcher?" Lisa asked, moving the interview onto territory she could control.

Dylan leaned back, rocking lightly. For a moment Lisa thought he was going to object.

"Go ahead, Miss Sterling," Dylan replied. Perry just nodded.

Lisa glanced down at the paper she'd brought to

help keep her on track. "Why did your current secretary leave?"

"She was going on maternity leave and then decided she wanted to stay home with her new baby instead of coming back to work."

That sounded reassuring. "You talked about trips. How often would you expect me to accompany you?"

"As long as I'm around, once a month to our Vancouver office. There might even be a couple of times Perry will need you to accompany him on overseas trips."

In spite of her initial hesitation at taking the job, she felt a frisson of excitement. Once a month to Vancouver? She could arrange to meet Gabe and talk to him face-to-face, rather than over the telephone. Try to talk some sense into him before his growing anger with Matheson Telecom pushed him to do something rash.

"Am I going to be working for both you and Mr. Hatcher?"

Dylan glanced at Perry as if seeking confirmation. "You would be working for me for about a month. After that, Mr. Hatcher will be taking over from me."

Lisa's mind raced, trying to fit in this new piece of information. She had figured on working for Dylan. Dylan's brother had been the one to fire Gabe— she had counted on using Dylan to find out what she needed. She couldn't accomplish that working for Perry.

Could she do that in the month Dylan was still here?

"Do you have any other questions?" Dylan asked.

"No. Just those few."

Dylan stopped swiveling. "Then, Miss Sterling, you're hired. It will become official after we've checked your references."

Lisa didn't even know how tense she'd been until she relaxed back against the chair. "Thank you very much," she said quietly, hoping her relief and her nervousness didn't show.

A month as Dylan's secretary might not be enough. But if she didn't take this job, she had no way of helping Gabe at all.

"Do you have any other questions for either myself or Perry?"

"Maybe you can give me a rough idea of what you expect from me?"

"That sounds like a good plan." Dylan smiled fully now, and Lisa was surprised at how it relaxed his features. Softened the hooded look of his eyes.

And for the span of a heartbeat she felt an unprofessional tug of attraction.

Don't even start, she warned herself, flipping open her notebook. He's your new boss. You're the secretary.

And he's the enemy.

Lisa pushed the drawer of the file cabinet shut with her fingertips, as if minimizing her contact with it. This was the second morning in a week she had come to the office early hoping to do some investigating without Dylan, Perry or the other office workers seeing her. She knew she couldn't expect to uncover anything major so soon. But she'd hoped to find more than she had. Which was nothing.

Dara, Dylan's sister-in-law, had called yesterday, wanting—no, demanding—to talk to Dylan, but he'd been away. When Lisa hung up, guilt had her heart thudding in her chest. Gabe had worked under Dara before he was fired.

Heavy footsteps in the hallway sent her scurrying to her desk. She sat at her computer—which was already on—looking busy with the file on her desk.

When Dylan came into the office she looked up with a careful smile. "Good morning, Mr. Matheson."

"Good morning, Lisa. You're here early."

Very early, she thought, stifling a yawn. To beat Dylan to the office she had to show up at least an hour and a half before the office opened. Tony was a hard worker, but not the workaholic Dylan seemed to be. "I had some work to catch up on, Mr. Matheson."

He stopped in front of her desk, angling her a quizzical grin. "Please call me Dylan."

In her mind she heard the echo of her previous boss. Please call me Tony. And she had. Bad move.

So she just nodded politely. As long as she was working for him he'd stay Mr. Matheson.

"Anything come up yesterday?"

"Your sister-in-law, Dara, called. She seemed to think I was putting her off when I told her you weren't available."

Dylan shrugged. "She can be quite insistent." He gave her another smile, one that softened the angles of his face.

Lisa couldn't help acknowledging his appeal. And that was why she'd never call him Dylan.

"I'm in all day today, though," he continued. "You won't have to put her off if she does call."

"Good enough." She glanced at the file folder on her desk, making it look more urgent than it was. Dylan waited a moment, then left.

"Your mother is on line two, Mr. Matheson."

Dylan shook his head at the official address. Since Lisa had started he'd been trying to get her to call him Dylan. Once in a while she'd slip, but for two weeks he'd been Mr. Matheson to her. Made him feel like his father.

He hit the intercom button. "Thanks, Lisa."

Then he sucked in a long, slow breath and picked up the phone.

"Hello, Mother."

"Dylan, darling. Your sister Chelsea tells me you won't be coming until Thursday evening. You'll miss the luncheon her future in-laws are having on Wednesday."

Trust his mother to dispense with the niceties and dive right in. "You mean we're not eating enough at the rehearsal party and at Chelsea and Jordan's wedding?"

Stephanie Matheson was silent a moment, as if trying to figure out what he'd said. "It's just a chance to get to know each other," she said finally, a sigh of displeasure sifting through her voice. "Just a small affair. Why can't you come?"

"I've already booked the flight, Mother." Dylan leaned back in his chair, massaging his forehead with his fingertips. The faint pressure was starting already. "I won't come any sooner."

"And you'll be staying at the house until the anniversary?"

"Of course." Not his choice, but staying in a hotel was not worth the gentle insurrection that would be staged by the combined forces of his sisters and his mother. He would have preferred a little more distance from his father. He would also have preferred to leave after the wedding. He had a ton of work to do before he left the company. He had an important meeting with his new partners the day of his return flight, but his parents' thirty-fifth anniversary was important and he knew he had to attend. Besides, it was sort of a swan song—the last time he would see his father as a partner in Matheson Telecom. When he came back, he would jump right into his new job.

So for the ten days they were going to be together, he and his father, Alex, would have to at least pretend to get along.

"That's wonderful. And of course you'll be bringing an escort to the wedding and our anniversary?"

Dread dropped on his shoulders.

When Chelsea had phoned to get his tuxedo size for the wedding she'd told him he had better bring his current girlfriend or she and his mother would find someone for him. However, since the phone call and the present moment, he and Felicia had broken up.

If he let his mother know he was coming alone now, she would be on the phone before it was cold in her hands, arranging, plotting and planning with her sisters and all the mothers of eligible daughters who were "so wonderful, Dylan."

A light knock at the door granted him a momentary respite.

"Just a moment, Mother," Dylan said, then laid his hand on the mouthpiece. "Come in."

Lisa entered, holding a sheaf of papers for him to sign. When she saw him on the phone she half turned as if to leave again, but he waved her in. "I'll just be a moment," he said quietly.

He tucked the phone under his chin and uncapped his pen.

"Amber and Erika wanted to have a welcome-home party after the wedding," his mother continued. "As if I have time. Honestly, those girls seem to think putting together a party is as easy as ordering coffee." Stephanie laughed lightly as Dylan's signature on the letters grew larger, bolder. His sisters organizing a party. Now, there was a scary proposition. Giggly girlfriends and heavy hints.

"Anyhow, they were wondering if your girlfriend was going to be coming with you. What's her name again?"

Dylan's pen dug into the page. "Felicia won't be coming." His ex-girlfriend's deceit still stung. That she had been seeing someone else had been bad enough. That it had been one of his employees made it worse.

Ex-employee, he amended.

"I told the girls you would probably come alone."

Dylan could practically feel his mother's spine stiffening. It wasn't enough that one sister had dutifully married young and provided his mother with grandchildren, that his brother was also married and that a second sister was going to make the trip down the aisle. Stephanie wanted to see Dylan settled, as well.

Trouble was, he had never found anyone who captivated him enough to take the chance. His mother was always telling him he looked in the wrong places. He wondered where the right ones were.

"I wouldn't worry about coming alone, son," his mother continued, her words coming out in a rush. "The girls invited some of their friends to the wedding. We've arranged for you to take one as an escort. Do you remember Kerry? Lovely girl. Goes to church. Just a sweet little thing."

The chill in his blood got colder.

Lisa removed the top letter so he could sign the one below.

"Mother, that's not necessary."

"I know you, Dylan. You'll come alone like you always do."

The slight edge in his mother's voice told him how serious she was about this. And what was in store for him if he didn't show up with someone. Anyone.

Dylan had sat through tough negotiations with rival companies, bluffed his way through contract negotiations with suppliers, all without losing his self-control. But his mother's desire to see him wed was an immovable force against which he had bumped time after time.

His headache grew with each passing moment. Showing up without somebody, *anybody,* to create a buffer between his mother, his sisters and his sisters' friends would create a nightmare.

Lisa took the signed letters from him.

"Excuse me a moment, Mother," he said. He looked up at his secretary. "Just wait, Lisa. I need to go over a few things with you."

"Oh, my goodness," he heard his mother say over the phone. "I'm sorry, Dylan. I didn't realize you were busy."

Dylan smiled at Lisa in apology for taking up her time. And gave her a second look. Her curly blond hair was tamed today, pulled back from her face in an intricate arrangement of pins. Funky without looking too offbeat. Her soft brown eyes were framed by thick lashes. Her high cheekbones were softened by the dimples lurking at the corners of her mouth. She smiled back, releasing the dimples.

And he felt a faint stirring of attraction.

Was he crazy? Hadn't he learned his lesson from Felicia?

"Well, then, we'll be seeing you Thursday evening?" his mother was asking.

Dylan pulled himself back to the reality of his mother and the conversation they were having.

"Of course," he said, leaning back in his chair.

"And your father really needs to talk to you about the business."

"I thought the problem with that accountant was dealt with."

"Not completely, I guess."

Lisa suddenly bent to gather the papers on his desk, then pointed over her shoulder at her office. He nodded. He could talk to her later. No telling how long his mother wanted to chat.

Then, as Lisa straightened, her eyes caught his, her gaze intent. And once again a frisson of awareness tingled through him.

Lisa usually avoided his gaze. Made minimal eye contact. As the door closed behind her, he wondered what had caused the change.

"Come as soon as you can, Dylan. Your father really needs to have you around." Stephanie paused, as if hoping Dylan would fill the momentary silence. But he wouldn't bite. If his father wanted him around, Alex could phone and say so himself. But he never did. "You take care of yourself, son," his mother was saying. "Love you."

Dylan echoed his mother's reply, then said goodbye. As he hung up, his eyes fell on the desk calendar his mother had given him. It was a pad with a Bible verse for every day. He hadn't looked at it for a month.

Yet he was looking at today's date. And today's verse. Maybe Lisa had kept it current.

Idly he turned the calendar toward him to read it better. "As a father has compassion on his children, so the Lord has compassion on those who fear Him" was the verse for the day. And that was just the trouble, wasn't it? His father's continuing compassion for one child in particular. Ted.

Charming, exuberant, unreliable Ted.

When Alex Matheson had approached Dylan five years ago to quit his successful job with a marketing firm and join Matheson Telecom, it was with the tantalizing promise that Dylan would be taking over the head office in Vancouver.

But when the time had come, his brother, Ted, had been given the reins of the company instead, with no explanation on his father's part. Dylan, angry with his father's betrayal of trust, had left to take over the Toronto branch of Matheson Telecom. He'd lost himself in his work, determined to prove his worth.

Since then the two of them spoke only when necessary.

The Toronto branch had done well, but Dylan chafed at the restraints put on him by his brother and father in the head office. When Dylan saw his father wasn't going to change anything, he started making his own plans and grooming Perry Hatcher to take over.

Dylan pushed away from his desk and strode to the window looking out over the Toronto harbor. He used to have a sailboat docked there, just a small sloop, but setting up this branch of the company took up all his extra time. That it was now more successful than the Vancouver branch was bittersweet proof to his father that Alex Matheson had made a mistake.

Now his father wanted him to come back and clean up behind Ted. And his mother wanted him to

come with an escort. If he didn't, he would have to
spend the entire visit home avoiding his sisters and
their friends.

This wasn't going to be much of a holiday after
all, he thought with a light sigh.

Lisa closed the door behind her and slowly blew
out a shaky breath.

When Dylan had mentioned ''accountant,'' her
heart had plunged. She was sure he was talking about
Gabe. And she was also sure from the way he'd
looked at her that guilt had been written all over her
face. What if he found out about her connection to
Gabe?

She didn't know how he could. She and Gabe had
different last names. When she had filled in the pa-
perwork for employment she hadn't marked the box
asking if any family members worked for Matheson
Telecom. Gabe had already been fired, so technically
he wasn't working for the company anymore.

She was too jumpy, that was all. If she wanted to
help Gabe, she'd have to perfect her innocent look.

Trouble was, Gabe's phone calls were starting to
frighten her. He had called again just last night, angry and frustrated.

She had tried to reason with him not to quit his
current job as a salesclerk. But he was feeling de-
pressed and wondering why he should bother doing
honest work when his employer didn't believe him.

Thankfully he had settled down when she'd told
him that she was working for Matheson Telecom.

That she would get to the bottom of what had happened. Gabe just needed to be patient.

Patience wasn't Gabe's strength. Ever since they'd been put into foster care after their parents died Lisa had watched out for Gabe. When she'd graduated from high school she got a job and an apartment and applied to have Gabe move in with her. Thankfully, Social Services had agreed.

In high school Gabe had started hanging out with a bad crowd. After a close brush with the law, Lisa had pulled him away from this rowdy group of boys, scared that Social Services might separate them. She had put her own life on hold to take care of him. To give him a chance. His graduation from college with a degree in accounting had been a celebration for Lisa and a validation of all the sacrifices she had made for him.

Now he sounded as if he was going to throw away everything she had done for him unless Lisa could find a way to clear his name. She had to find a way to get to Vancouver, she thought. Had to find a way to help him. He was the only family she had now.

Settling down in front of her computer, she opened the most recent file and began typing, her fingers still trembling from the close call a few moments earlier. The routine of the work slowly eased her jitters, so that when Dylan emerged from his office at the end of the day she was fully in control.

He stopped in front of her desk, dominating the space with his presence. His tie was loosened, the sleeves of his shirt rolled up, giving him a casually vulnerable air. "I wanted to ask you if you've got that spreadsheet done."

Lisa looked up at him, her secretary smile in place. "Almost, Mr. Matheson. So if you want to wait a moment, I can show you the sales figures."

"Please, just Dylan." He scratched his forehead with an index finger, looking hesitant. "It's past five o'clock. Why are you still here?"

Because she was hoping to look through some more files when he was gone. She had so little time with Dylan still around. She was starting to feel a little panicky. In less than a month he would be gone, and she still hadn't found anything substantial.

"Just like to get done."

"Very dedicated." He crossed his arms over his chest, his head tilted to one side as he looked at her.

"Is there something else you wanted?" she asked, her heart kicking up shards of guilt. She just wanted him to go.

He sat down in the chair across from her desk, as if he was settling in for a chat. "Yes. I want to stay here and avoid my sister's wedding and my parents' anniversary."

"Why would you want to do that?" Lisa was surprised at his sudden disclosure. In the past week he had been polite, but a bit distant. Just the way she liked it.

"Because if I go, my mother is going to play matchmaker and I'm going to end up trying to avoid yet another sweet but boring young lady." Dylan sighed, rubbing his hand over his face.

"Why don't you find someone yourself?"

"I should," Dylan said heavily. "But I'm going to be so busy with company business while I'm there that anyone I take would be sitting around while I dealt with that."

An impulse jumped into her mind. She needed to get to Vancouver. In less than a month Dylan, and her one solid connection to the Matheson company, was going to be gone. It was the perfect opportunity, and before she could even think about it, she spoke. "I could go with you. Help you with your father's problem. Pose as your girlfriend. Could cover two things in one easy solution."

Dylan's head snapped up. He stared at her a moment, then nodded, a grin crawling along his lips. "You know, that would be a great idea. I think it could work just perfectly."

Lisa beat down a flurry of nerves.

Vancouver. Already.

She didn't want to think about the implications of attending the wedding as Dylan's escort. She'd deal with that as it came. For now, she'd have an opportunity to meet his family. And maybe, just maybe, his work would involve the conversation he'd had with his mother in his office this morning. Things were starting to come together quite nicely.

"I'll have to phone my mom and tell her," Dylan said, pushing himself to his feet.

Lisa frowned. "Tell her what?"

"To make up an extra bedroom. I usually stay at my parents' place."

Sleeping with the enemy. Lisa pulled in a steadying breath. "Okay. I'll let you arrange that, then."

Lisa turned back to her computer, quelling a sudden rush of nerves. This was a good thing, she reminded herself. Staying at the Matheson house would bring her closer to the family and any potential source of information.

"One more thing, Lisa."

She turned to him, her smile cautious.

"Pack something dressy for the wedding and the anniversary party." Dylan gave her a crooked smile, then left.

Second thoughts swirled through her mind as Dylan closed the door behind him. With each request he made she felt pushed into an ever-shrinking corner.

What had she done? Bad enough that she was working for him under false pretenses. Now she was going to Vancouver burdened with even more.

Don't think about it. You're doing this all because of Gabe.

And staying that close to Dylan?

That thought crept into the part of her mind that couldn't help acknowledging Dylan's appeal. His good looks.

She quashed the idea ruthlessly. Dylan was her boss. And part of the company that had falsely accused her brother.

And if she didn't want a repeat of Tony, she would do well to keep her professional distance.

Chapter Two

The runway flew past her window. Lisa's exhilaration built with the speed of the plane. Then she was pressed back against the seat as the front of the plane lifted off the ground, the city of Toronto dropping away from them.

Point of no return.

Anxiety trembled through Lisa. No time for second thoughts. She was on her way.

Lisa glanced at her seatmate. Dylan casually thumbed through a magazine as if he was sitting in his living room rather than within a thousand tons of steel hurtling through the air.

When Lisa had phoned Gabe to tell him she was coming to Vancouver, his skepticism had fed her nervousness and planted the seeds of second thoughts.

She shook them off. If she was careful, there was no reason the Mathesons or Dylan should discover her plan. And if she was right, her actions would be vindicated.

And how do you fit this with the promise you made in Dylan's office? To go to church if you got this job?

Whatever your lips utter you must be sure to do. The thought slipped into her mind, ringing with clarity. Gabe's father used to laughingly quote this passage from the Old Testament laws whenever Lisa made one of her many extravagant promises.

Lisa and her mother didn't go to church until Trish met and married Gabe's father. Rick Haskell introduced Lisa and Trish to church. And God. They went regularly and Lisa attended Bible classes, eagerly absorbing the teachings.

But after the accident that killed Lisa's mother and Gabe's father, Lisa's faith took a blow. She didn't trust God, and neither she nor Gabe had attended church since.

Dylan glanced up and caught her gaze. "How are you doing?"

"Good." She looked away, out the window at the patchwork of fields and roads spread out below her, pushing her doubts and her guilt aside. "This is quite a rush. Flying."

"You don't fly often?"

Lisa quelled her embarrassment. "Actually, this is my maiden flight."

Dylan was silent, and she couldn't help looking over to check his reaction.

His gray-blue eyes held hers, his mouth pulled up in a half smile. "You've never flown before?"

"I know it's an anomaly in this peripatetic age, but no, I've never flown before."

"Well then, we're even." His half smile was full-blown now, crinkling the corners of his eyes, softening the austerity of his features.

Lisa frowned. "How do you figure that?"

"I've never heard words like *anomaly* and *peripatetic* used in the same sentence."

She laughed. "Sorry. That's a holdover from a game I used to play with my stepfather and…" Just in time she caught herself from saying Gabe's name. "And he used to challenge me to find unusual words," she amended, stifling her beating heart. "Then use them as often as possible in one day."

"Where is your stepfather now?"

"He died ten years ago."

"And your mother?"

"She died at the same time." The flicker of sorrow caught her by surprise. It had been a long time since anyone had asked about her parents. A long time since anyone had cared.

"I'm sorry to hear that. You must have been about fifteen when that happened. Where did you go then?"

"Foster home." She looked down at her hands, twined tightly on her lap. Each question of Dylan's probed places in her life that still felt painfully tender, even after all the years. And they created a discomfort she wanted to deflect. Well offense was the best defense. "What about your family? What are they like? Busy? Happy? I guess I should know, if I'm supposed to be attending as your escort."

Dylan held her gaze, his expression intent. As if he knew she was avoiding his questions. But thankfully he simply smiled and rubbed his chin. "My parents' names are Stephanie and Alex Matheson. Married thirty-five years."

"Hold on a minute." Lisa pulled a pad of paper and a pen out of her briefcase. "I think I might need to write this down."

"Always the secretary," murmured Dylan.

"That is my job, Mr. Matheson," she said, scribbling down his parents' names.

A strong finger pressed down on her pad of paper, catching her attention.

"Since you're also my escort slash girlfriend, it would look better if you called me Dylan." He smiled again, his eyes holding hers.

Lisa couldn't look away. She could lose herself in those eyes. More gray now, soft and inviting.

She blinked, breaking the insidious spell he seemed to be weaving.

"Okay." She tossed him a smile, then looked back down at the pad of paper. "You mentioned your parents. Tell me about the rest of your family."

"They're just family. You'll meet them one at a time."

"And I'll forget them the same way. A computer I'm not."

Dylan shrugged, and Lisa sensed in him the same reticence she had just displayed. For a moment she thought he wasn't going to say anything.

"My mother's name is Stephanie, as I said, and she doesn't stand on formality, either. My father is

Alex. Tiffany is younger than me and looks the most like me," he said. "She's married to Arnold. They have two children, Justin and Tammy. Chelsea is twenty-five, pretty, but then I'm prejudiced. It's her wedding we'll be attending. After her come twin sisters, Erika and Amber, unmarried, with more single girlfriends than Solomon had wives. Sometimes they live at home, sometimes they rent an apartment downtown. I'm not sure what it is this month."

"Sounds like you're a very lucky man." Lisa couldn't keep the light note of envy from her voice. "All those sisters."

"I also have a brother. Ted."

Lisa looked up from her scribbling, her heart skipping at the sound of his brother's name. The man who had fired Gabe. "And where is he?"

"Ted is married to Dara. He is a partner with my father in the company." His hands, clutching the armrests of his seat, betrayed the emotion his voice and expression held back. Then he glanced at her, loosening his tie and unbuttoning the top button of his shirt. "And that's my family."

Lisa put the pad of paper away and looked out the window, sensing they weren't going to be talking much anymore. It seemed they both had their secrets.

"I called my mother, and she's expecting us for supper," Dylan said, slipping his cell phone into his briefcase.

"Supper?" Lisa's heart did a slow flip in her chest. "Already?"

"I guess they're anxious to meet you," he said with a sardonic lift of his mouth.

Lisa stifled another attack of nerves as they walked to the gleaming row of rental cars, their footsteps echoing hollowly in the concrete car park. "Wow, meeting parents," she said lightly as Dylan unlocked the trunk of the car. "Something else to add to my 'things I've never done before' file."

"No boyfriends you dated that wanted you to meet Mom and Dad?" Dylan asked, dropping their suitcases into the back.

"No parents to reciprocate."

Dylan held her gaze, his expression growing serious. "I'm sorry. That was unforgivable. I had forgotten."

"It's okay. With your family you probably can't imagine someone going it alone in the world." She didn't want to sound whiney and hoped her flippant tone would put him at ease.

"So how long has it been since you've been back home?" Lisa asked when they were settled in the car.

"About half a year." Dylan glanced over his shoulder as he reversed the car out of the parking lot. "I usually go home more. My sisters and my mother have come to visit me a few times in Toronto."

"So what's been keeping you away this time?"

Dylan's only response was a shrug. Another mystery.

He switched lanes, sped up and switched again, the traffic becoming more congested and busier as they entered the canyon of buildings in the downtown core.

Then buildings fell away, trees loomed ahead and within seconds they were speeding through silent, dark woods.

"Is this Stanley Park?" she asked, twisting in her seat to get a closer look at the decades-old trees forming a lush canopy above and beyond. "Right in the middle of the city like this?"

"One of Vancouver's true beauties," Dylan said. "You could spend a couple of days just walking around this park."

"I might have to try that someday," Lisa said, trying to take in the size of the trees, the depth of the forest. It looked cool, inviting. Secretive.

A young couple walked along one of the paths, pushing a stroller, a younger child in shorts and a T-shirt bouncing ahead of them. Sunlight filtered through the trees, dappling their figures. A family.

Lisa watched them, turning her head as they fell behind, envy surprising her. Then Dylan rounded a curve and they were hidden from view.

She turned, watching the approaching bridge, the two lions guarding the entrance. Suspension wires swept gracefully between two pillars. The bridge went on, higher and longer. Far below them she saw large ships and barges pulled by squat tugboats. Sailboats fluttered amongst them like ballet dancers weaving through a pack of wrestlers.

She craned her neck to see better, watching as the boats slipped through the water. "What a beautiful sight."

"Ever sail before?" Dylan asked.

Lisa shook her head. "Never."

"I'll have to take you in the family's boat if we have time."

"Your family has its own sailboat?"

Dylan threw her a puzzled frown. "Yes."

The tone in his voice implied an "of course." As if it was the most natural thing in the world for a family to own something as luxurious as their own boat. Lisa had never even owned her own car until she had paid off Gabe's and her student loans. And that car was a fourth- or maybe even fifth-hand beater.

Sailboats, in her mind, were equated with the very upper class. A group of people who moved in a world far beyond her everyday reality.

She swallowed down a flutter of nerves.

Dylan followed the freeway, bordered, as well, by trees. He swung off onto an exit and soon they were climbing another hill, the road twisting back on itself. The higher they went, the more expansive the view behind them and the larger the homes.

When Dylan finally turned into a curved driveway bordered by a stone fence, Lisa couldn't help but stare at the sight that greeted her. The house soared three stories above her, all glass and lines and cantilevered levels. A glassed-in balcony swept along the front, following the curve of the huge bow window that broke the austere lines of the house. The same balcony was echoed one floor below, but smaller. The entire building was a stark white against the deep green of the cedar trees surrounding it on two sides, dark and mysterious.

"Ugly, isn't it?" Dylan said dryly as he parked in front of one of the doors of a four-car garage. "The house, I mean. Mom has always dreamed of designing and building her own home. So my father bought this lot, and found a contractor willing to work with Mom. Together they created this monstrosity."

"It's very impressive," she said cautiously.

"Mom paid for impressive. You'll have to tell her so."

"If it's something she designed herself, then it's amazing."

Dylan looked down at her, his expression softening. A faint smile crawled across his lips, deepening the line that ran from his nose to one corner of his mouth. "Tell her that and she'll fall in love with you," he said.

Lisa couldn't look away and he didn't. Love? From a mother? That had been a while, she thought with a twinge of sorrow. And what would your mother say about the deception you're playing now?

She pushed the thought resolutely aside and was about to get out of the car when Dylan laid his hand on her arm. She pulled back.

"If we're supposed to be together, you might want to avoid avoiding me like that," Dylan said with a faint smile.

"Sorry." Lisa felt silly. It was just a casual touch, yet it had sent a tingle up her arm.

"I feel I should warn you about a few things before we go in. I have never brought any of my girlfriends home to meet my parents yet. The fact that I'm bringing you here will make them suspicious. And when my sisters and mother get suspicious, they get nosy. I hope to head them off when possible, but don't be surprised if they ask you a bunch of questions.''

''Like how we met?''

''We'll tell them we met at work.''

He sighed lightly, drumming his fingers on the steering wheel.

''I'm guessing there's more?'' Lisa said, prompting him.

''Yes. Every time I've mentioned a girl to them they always ask me if she's a Christian.'' He waved his hand as if dismissing their concerns. ''Don't be surprised if that comes up somewhere in the conversation. I know we're technically not 'together,' but they don't know that.''

''Don't worry. I think I can handle myself.''

''That's what I was hoping. I'll get the suitcases.''

Lisa gave him a bright smile, which faded as she got out of the car. Deeper and deeper, she thought with a flash of panic.

It's just a game, she reminded herself. Just a game.

She took a deep breath and followed Dylan up the stone walkway to the main entrance of the house.

The double oak doors at the top burst open and two young women launched themselves at Dylan. He dropped the suitcases just as they grabbed him.

''Dylan, you came.''

''We've been waiting and waiting.''

''Chelsea thought you wouldn't show.''

"How was your flight? How are you? It's been ages."

The words fluttered around them as the girls clutched Dylan's arms, bracketing him like matching bookends.

The twin sisters, Lisa guessed as she watched the exuberant reunion. Their short caps of dark brown hair were the same shade as Dylan's. Where he was tall, they were of slight build, coming only to his shoulder. They wore matching hip hugging blue jeans, artfully faded. One topped them with a bell-sleeved shirt in peach, the other a fitted T-shirt and a wooden beaded necklace.

One of the girls stood on tiptoe to kiss Dylan soundly on the cheek. "We've missed you, big brother."

"I missed you, too, Erika."

Dylan turned to Lisa, beckoning for her to come forward.

She steeled herself for the all-too-familiar tightening of her stomach. How many times had she endured these "first meetings" in the many families she'd been brought to? The acknowledgments, the reserve that always greeted her. The moment of awkwardness, the hard work that accompanied all these initial moments.

It's just a game, she reminded herself again, angry with her nervousness. You don't need their approval. She took a slow breath and smiled.

"Erika. Amber. I'd like you to meet Lisa Sterling," Dylan said, turning toward her. "My…girlfriend."

Dylan's use of the term reminded her of the role she was playing.

Years of experience made Lisa lift her chin and take a few more steps up the stairs to come to Erika and Amber's level. She met their quizzical gazes head-on.

Then, to her utter surprise, she felt Dylan slip his arm around her waist. Pull her close to him.

He was almost as much of a stranger as his sisters were, yet she felt a curious sense of being protected. Cared for.

Don't be silly, she reminded herself with a jolt. It's just part of the show. But she didn't pull away.

"Lisa, I'd like you to meet my sisters, Amber and Erika. The easiest way to tell them apart is to remember that Erika is the more talkative one."

"Thanks a lot, Dylan. Perfect introduction for us. I hate to think what you told her on the trip up. She's going to think we're a couple of airheads. Which we're not." The twin in the peach angora sweater pouted at her brother, then turned back to Lisa. "I'm Erika."

Lisa caught Dylan's knowing smirk and tried not to smile.

"Welcome to our home, Lisa," Amber said, shaking Lisa's hand, as well. "Mom told us you're Dylan's secretary. I hope he doesn't make you work too hard while you're here."

"Come on, you make me sound like an ogre," Dylan said with a laugh, pulling his sister to his side.

"Kerry is coming over later," Erika said, giving her brother a gentle punch. "She's looking forward to seeing you. And Ted and Dara wanted to come by, too.''

''Isn't that nice.'' Dylan dropped a light kiss on his sister's head, his smile forced.

Then to Lisa's relief he let go of her. She followed the girls into the house, Dylan behind her.

White and light and angles was her first impression. A boldly colorful print dominated the wall above the sweeping staircase. A single metal sculpture glinted at her from an alcove below the stairs.

It wasn't just a house, she realized, her footsteps echoing in the wide-open foyer. It was a showcase.

''Cozy, isn't it?'' Dylan's sardonic voice broke in to her thoughts.

''It has its own beauty,'' Lisa said, awed by the space captured by just the entrance.

''Dylan hates this house,'' Amber said with a laugh. ''He's still complaining that Mom and Dad sold our other place.''

''That house had personality. I feel like I should be under anesthetic when I come here,'' Dylan groused.

As Lisa followed Dylan's sisters down the spacious hallway, she caught a glimpse of what must be a living room with tall windows, gray furniture and ocher accents. A set of French doors to her right showed her a room done up in darker tones. Den? Library? She didn't have time to take it in. Erika and Amber kept walking, going past another set of doors to yet another room and finally turning a corner into a large open kitchen area.

Light poured into the room from windows two

floors high. A white table, already set with yellow place mats and gleaming white-and-blue china, was tucked into one corner of the room. Plants softened the brightness here, adding a warmth absent in the rest of the house.

Through a large expanse of glass Lisa saw another view of the landscaped gardens, and beyond that a breathtaking vista of Burrard Inlet bisected by the bridge they had gone over and edged by the hazy skyline of downtown Vancouver.

Money, was the first word that slipped into her mind. Money enough to pay for all this.

Lisa pushed down a flurry of panic. In what dream world had she hatched her silly scheme to try to bring justice for her stepbrother against this family? A family with enough money to build a home whose cost she couldn't even begin to calculate.

"Dylan, how are you?"

Lisa took a calming breath and turned to see an elegantly clad woman step around the counter, her arms out to Dylan.

"Hello, Mother."

Lisa was surprised at the warmth in Dylan's voice and the note of yearning in his mother's. She found she couldn't look away, a bittersweet pain clenching her heart as she watched Dylan enfolded in a warm embrace, his arms encircling his mother's shoulders.

"I missed you, son," Dylan's mother said, her hands stroking his thick hair, her eyes taking in his features as if she was seeing him for the first time.

This was Stephanie Matheson, Lisa reminded herself, as if remembering a school lesson.

Dylan gave his mother another hug, then turned to Lisa, gesturing for her to come near. She was surprised at the clench of nerves tightening her stomach. Being a guest in this amazing home brought to a head what she had gotten herself into. Suddenly it was not only Dylan she was trying to fool. Now it was sisters, parents. Family.

The plan that had seemed so straightforward back in Toronto now took on an ominous note.

"Lisa, this is my mother, Stephanie Matheson."

Lisa held out her hand, keeping her smile intact as she met eyes the same piercing gray-blue as Dylan's.

"Welcome to our house, Lisa. I'm so glad you don't mind staying here." As Stephanie took Lisa's hand, she tipped her head to one side, as if conducting her own interview.

Lisa took Stephanie's hand in hers and shook it firmly, holding her gaze measure for measure. Think of Gabe, she thought. You're here because of Gabe.

But when she let go of Stephanie's hand, she chanced a quick glance at Dylan, surprised to see him studying her with a faint smile on his face.

She looked away. She couldn't afford to get distracted. So Dylan had a family. That shouldn't matter.

She was here to take care of her own family.

Chapter Three

Dylan pushed the sleeves of his sweater up his arms and gave himself a quick inspection in the mirror. Could use a haircut. He ran his hand over the shadow on his jaw. Probably should have shaved. He was looking a little scruffy.

And why did he care? He certainly never worried about how he looked in front of his family. He was sure Lisa wouldn't notice.

He stepped out of the bedroom and walked down the hall. The door to Lisa's room was open. He heard her voice.

His sisters were being surprisingly friendly, he thought, knocking lightly on the door. He pushed it open farther, but Lisa sat with her back to him, talking on a cell phone.

Feeling foolish, he was about to leave when she glanced over her shoulder. Her eyes grew wide and she quickly snapped the phone shut.

"Sorry," Dylan said. "I thought you were talking to one of my sisters."

Lisa shook her head, dropped the phone into her open briefcase on the bed, then clicked the case shut. "No, I was just…just checking…my messages."

She didn't look up at him, which puzzled Dylan even more. Why was she looking so guilty about checking her phone messages?

"Is everything okay?" he asked. "With the room?"

She got up, flashing him a quick smile. "It's lovely. Much nicer and much larger than a hotel room."

"I thought I should let you know that we should head down for dinner."

"Should I have changed?" Lisa glanced down at the narrow skirt she had worn on the airplane.

"You look fine." He didn't know of too many women who could come off a four-hour flight and look so fresh. Her skirt was barely wrinkled and her shirt looked as crisp as when they'd boarded. "I just changed because I get tired of wearing a suit."

"Okay. I suppose we should go, then." But as she passed him he heard the muffled ringing of her cell phone.

"Do you want to get that?" he asked as she spun around.

"No. No." Lisa waved her hand as if dismissing the call. "He can leave a message." She flashed him a quick smile, then left the room, leaving Dylan no choice but to follow her. And wonder how she knew it was a ''he'' that was calling.

And why she didn't answer it.

The wave of laughter that rolled down the hallway from the kitchen was a stark contrast to the panic clenching Lisa's stomach.

That had been too close. She had been so anxious to connect with Gabe that she hadn't thought to shut the bedroom door. When she'd heard the phone ringing again, she'd known it was him calling her back, which had sent her heart up into her throat.

''Lisa. Wait a minute.''

She swallowed and turned to face Dylan, praying the guilt she felt wasn't written all over her face.

''You're losing a hairpin.'' As he reached up to catch it, his warm fingers brushed her neck. She jerked her head back, feeling immediately foolish.

''I'm sorry,'' she said, biting her lip as she took the pin from him. ''I'm not usually this jumpy.'' The phone call was a lesson to her. If she had to connect with Gabe, better do it away from this home. Being in the very home of the people she wanted to investigate put her at a disadvantage.

As she slipped the pin into her hair, she felt the urge to pray. To ask for help as she floundered through this uncomfortable situation.

''It's okay. My family can seem intimidating, but they're not.'' Dylan tipped his head, as if studying her. ''Just be yourself, only yourself as my date. I think they'll like you.''

His faint smile should have smoothed away her disquiet. Instead it created more anxiety. She wasn't supposed to have any relationship with this family.

"There you are." Stephanie paused in the doorway of the kitchen, holding a steaming dish, an apron covering her skirt. "Why don't you two stop chit-chatting and join us?"

Stephanie's comment made it sound as if she had caught them lingering. And again Lisa felt a warm flush rise up her neck.

"Well, I suppose we should get going, then," Dylan said with a smile. "I'll lead the way."

The first person Lisa saw was an older version of Dylan leaning back against the counter, flipping through a magazine. Alex Matheson, Lisa presumed.

But where Dylan's hair was dark, Alex's was sprinkled with gray. And where Dylan's eyes were a hard gray-blue, his father's were a softer shade of hazel.

He glanced up as they came closer, a broad smile brightening his face.

Dylan acknowledged his father's presence with a curt nod in greeting, then turned away as if a necessary but tiresome obligation had been dealt with. But as he did, Lisa caught a flash of pain in his father's eyes.

Dylan walked over to a young woman sitting at the table looking intently at a bridal magazine. "Kind of late to be changing your mind, Chels."

The woman looked up, then jumped off her chair, nearly upsetting it. "You made it. You came." She threw her arms around his neck, squeezing him tight.

"You can let go of me, or you're going to be out one groomsman." Dylan pulled back from his sister's exuberant embrace, but kept his arm around her waist.

Dylan turned to Lisa. "Chelsea, I'd like you to meet Lisa."

Lisa held out her hand, feeling more like a fraud with each family member she met.

Chelsea took her hand, giving Lisa a quick nod and a welcoming smile, then gave her brother a little dig in the ribs. "You know, you're the first…woman associated with Dylan that this family has ever met."

"I'm sure Lisa needs to know that," Dylan said with a shake of his head. "And this is my father, Alex." Dylan's voice lost the note of loving warmth when he introduced his father, and again Lisa wondered at the rift between them.

"Nice to meet you, Lisa," Alex said, taking her hand in both of his and squeezing it tight. "Welcome to our family."

To Lisa's surprise, she felt a lump forming in her throat at his greeting and the warm and welcoming smile he bestowed on her. They didn't know her at all, yet she felt as if she was being accepted like a fellow family member.

"Thank you," she said, suddenly short of words.

"And with the twins is their friend Kerry." Lisa turned to face a smiling young woman bracketed by the twins. But Kerry had eyes only for Dylan. "Hello, Dylan," Kerry said, her voice low. And sweet.

Lisa got an inkling of Dylan's dilemma and felt a flash of pity.

"We're not late, are we?" Another female voice

behind them made Dylan's head snap up, his eyes
narrowing as a chorus of hellos greeted this new ar-
rival.

Curious, Lisa turned around. A tall, willowy brunette wearing an eye-catching red shift entered the
room. Following her was a man of about the same
height, wearing a suit and tie.

"Hello, everyone." The brunette paused at Alex's
side, leaning sideways to brush a kiss near his cheek.
"How are you, Dad?" She didn't wait for a reply,
but turned to Dylan. "So the prodigal son has returned." She reached Dylan, but he didn't echo her
greeting. Nor did he raise his arms to her as she did
to him.

"I didn't know you and Ted were coming."

Lisa's heart plunged.

Would Dara recognize her as Gabe's stepsister?
Her mind raced backward, wondering if she had ever
sent Gabe a picture of herself. The man beside her
must be Ted. Dylan's brother.

Lisa felt suddenly exposed and panicky. She tried
not to shift behind Dylan. To hide.

But so far Dara had eyes only for Dylan, and Ted
was ignoring them both. "Your mother told me you
were going to be here, so I thought I would surprise
you." Dara laid her hand on Dylan's shoulder, giving
him a light shake. "So, surprise."

But Dylan didn't look surprised. Nor did he look
as pleased as Dara sounded.

Dylan shifted away from her, looking toward Lisa.
"Dara, Ted, I'd like you to meet Lisa Sterling, my

date.'' Lisa felt her heart jump at the last two words. It sounded so final.

Dara's hand slid down from Dylan's shoulder as she slowly turned around. Her brown eyes narrowed, zeroing in on Lisa.

Here it comes, thought Lisa, her heart jumping like a kangaroo. She tried to smile. Tried to look casual.

But before Dara could speak, Ted reached past his wife and shook Lisa's hand, his smile far more welcoming than Dara's.

''This is a first for us,'' Ted said with a light laugh. ''Nice to finally meet one of Dylan's girlfriends.''

''Supper's ready,'' Stephanie Matheson announced, bringing a large casserole dish to the table. ''Dylan, you can sit on the far corner of the table. Lisa, I've put you beside Dylan.'' Stephanie's smile held the same warmth that Alex's had. And as Lisa sat at the table, second and third and even fourth thoughts assailed her.

She should have taken Dylan's offer of a hotel. It would have been better for her and Gabe if she had maintained a distance from this family.

She hadn't expected to meet Dara and Ted this soon. Nor had she expected to like this family. It created a confusion she couldn't dismiss.

''You should sit on the end, Kerry.'' Amber moved over from her place kitty-corner from Dylan. Amber flashed Lisa an apologetic look. ''Kerry's left-handed.''

Lisa returned Amber's smile, but couldn't help notice the way Kerry eyed Dylan.

The bustle died down as everyone sat at the table.

Stephanie took her husband's hand and gave it a light shake. "Will you pray, Alex?"

Alex shook his head.

Lisa could see a faint line crease Stephanie's forehead. It disappeared as she glanced around the table with a light smile, then everyone bowed their heads. At the last moment Lisa realized what was happening and dropped her head, as well.

She closed her eyes as Dylan's mother began praying.

"We come to You, Lord, in humbleness of heart and praise You for the lives you have given us. Thank You, Lord, for safety in travels. For the food we can eat and enjoy together. Thank You too, for Lisa and Dylan's visit…"

Lisa felt a slow melancholy wrap itself around her heart. How long had it been since she had heard the sincere prayer of a believer? How long had it been since she'd heard anyone pray for her?

Stephanie's prayer was a reminder of what she had pushed out of her life in bitterness. A knot caught in her throat.

Then, thankfully, the prayer was over. Around her Dylan's family broke into a flurry of conversation. Lisa kept her head bowed a moment, shoring up her scattershot emotions.

"Sorry about that." Dylan's quiet voice beside her made her look up. He was looking down at her, a bemused expression on his face. "I hope you weren't too uncomfortable?"

Lisa shook her head. "It's been a while since I've prayed before meals."

"You used to?"

"Yes, when…" She stopped talking. Nothing personal, she reminded herself, turning to the salad in front of her.

"And what are you two plotting?" Dara asked, leaning forward to catch their attention, but it was Dylan who had her eye. "Takeover schemes? How to rescue the company?"

Again Lisa felt her face flush at Dara's implication.

"I'm sorry," Dylan said smoothly. "I didn't mean to look like we had secrets." And thankfully he said no more than that.

"So, Lisa, how did you meet Dylan?" Amber asked, her voice full of innocent inquiry.

"In the office." Lisa decided to play this as straightforward as she could.

"Convenient," Dara said.

"Yes, it is," Lisa returned, determined not to let this woman bulldoze her. "I guess I got a little more than I bargained for when I applied for the job."

Dylan's sidelong grin and wink was one of coconspirator, and the connection created a quiver of awareness.

"I thought you made it a rule never to get involved with your office staff," Amber said with a touch of petulance. She seemed to sense that Kerry was out of the running.

"And I hear you've been spending time with a certain hockey player, Amber," Dylan added. "Something I remember hearing you say you'd never do."

The blush on Amber's face evoked a wave of laughter.

Though Dylan had neatly parried Amber's obvious schemes, Erika didn't seem ready to give up their championing of Kerry as potential partner for Dylan. "Did we tell you, Dylan? Kerry works for that company that manufactures the newest in e-books. Kerry, tell Dylan about the new one you're working on."

Kerry's face lit up. She scooped her streaked blond hair behind her ear, her blue eyes fairly sparkling. Though she liked to dress well, Lisa was seldom self-conscious of her appearance. But being confronted with Kerry's beauty-queen good looks, she felt like a frump.

"E-books have been vastly underrated," Kerry said, leaning forward, her shining lips parted in a smile wide enough to show her perfectly aligned teeth. "But we've come up with a platform that makes the possibilities for our e-book wider than most of the limited-use, dedicated devices that have come up in the past." Kerry kept her eyes on Dylan, her smile coy as she absently toyed with her long hair.

"How does this relate to Matheson Telecom?"

"It could make a good addition to our product line," Dara put in, her smile competing with Kerry's.

"I think we've spread ourselves far enough," Dylan said, stabbing his salad with his fork.

"Dara might be right," Ted put in. "A company that doesn't move ahead goes behind."

"From the looks of things, we're doing that already," Dylan said, tension entering his voice.

"I don't think we need to talk business at the supper table," Stephanie said with a tight smile. "Chelsea, have you gotten hold of the caterers to finalize details?"

The conversation turned back to the wedding, leaving Lisa wondering again at the tension that existed between Dylan, his father and his brother.

The rest of the meal was a sparring match of words and jokes, half-finished sentences. Laughter was the dominant emotion. And questions. But after Stephanie's quiet warning, no business was spoken.

As she tried to eat, Lisa couldn't keep up with half the conversations, but she didn't mind. Far easier to be simply a silent bystander.

She noticed that in spite of the general air of togetherness around the table, Dylan and his father exchanged no more than a few sentences. Though Dylan hardly looked at his father, Alex's eyes were constantly on his son as if hoping for some connection.

"Have we met before, Lisa?" Dara asked suddenly. "The more I see you, the more familiar you seem."

Lisa kept her smile in place even as icy fingers tickled her spine. "My mother always told me my face was a dime a dozen. Maybe that's why."

Dara laughed lightly. "Maybe." But Lisa could tell Dara wasn't satisfied with the reply.

Lisa folded her napkin and laid it on her plate. She felt suddenly ill and wanted to leave. But she didn't want to be the first away from the table.

She looked up to see Alex watching her, a light frown on his face. Surely he didn't recognize her, as well?

Lisa steeled herself for another round of questions.

"I think we should finish this meal, Stephanie," Alex said, much to her relief. "We can have dessert in the living room."

He pulled a large worn book from a shelf behind him that was part of the kitchen cabinets. Lisa recognized a Bible. A well-read Bible.

He handed it to Stephanie.

"Why don't you read, dear?" she said softly.

He shook his head. With a slight nod of acquiescence, Stephanie took the book and paged through it. As she did, arms were crossed, faces turned toward her as a feeling of waiting permeated the room. This was normal routine, Lisa realized, sitting back in her chair.

"We always have devotions after our meal," Stephanie said, smiling at Lisa. "If you're uncomfortable with that, you are welcome to leave."

"No, this is fine." She glanced around the table, underlining her lack of objection. "Please, go ahead."

"Instead of reading through our usual devotions, I thought I would simply read a psalm." Stephanie glanced up at Lisa as she slipped her reading glasses on. "So that Lisa doesn't feel completely out of the loop."

Lisa felt that way already, but she simply smiled her thanks.

"Psalm thirty-three." Stephanie brushed a strand of hair back from her face and began to read. "'Sing joyfully to the Lord, you righteous; it is fitting for the upright to praise him....'"

The cadences and rhythms of the psalm washed over Lisa. Familiar enough that she could almost hear Rick Haskell's voice reading the words. A light pain settled in her chest, an echo of the one she'd felt in the airplane. Just like this family, Rick used to read the Bible after supper. Sometimes in the evening, as well. Unbidden, her thoughts returned to the angry place she revisited each time she thought of their deaths.

"'From heaven the Lord looks down and sees all mankind; from His dwelling place He watches all who live on earth, He who forms the hearts of all, who considers everything they do.'"

If God could truly see everyone, why had He taken Rick and her mother away from her and Gabe? What had they done to deserve such a loss?

"'We wait in hope for the Lord; He is our help and our shield. In Him our hearts rejoice, for we trust His holy name. May Your unfailing love rest upon us, O Lord, even as we put our hope in You.'"

As Stephanie read the last words of the psalm, Lisa lowered her head. How could she put her hope in

God? In the past few years the one thing she had discovered was that if she didn't take care of herself, no one else would.

Stephanie closed the Bible, and Lisa once again caught the appeal in her glance as she looked to her husband. But again he shook his head. Was this his job? Lisa wondered.

Stephanie glanced around the table, then lowered her head and began to pray. And against her will Lisa felt a gentle urging, a faint voice calling her.

Whatever your lips utter you must be sure to do.

She bit her lip, thinking of her silly bargain with God. But she was a person of her word, and she would find a chance to go to church.

But first she needed to get out of this house. It was too risky staying here.

And it was too hard being in the middle of this obviously happy and close family.

Dylan paused in front of Lisa's door. It was slightly ajar and the light shone through the opening into the hallway. He should just keep going, but he wanted to make sure she was okay. She'd seemed a little jumpy at suppertime.

He knocked lightly on the door.

"Who is it?"

"Me. Dylan."

He heard a rustling sound and then she was at the door. She had changed into sweatpants and a hooded sweatshirt, her hair now hanging loose over her shoulders. The casual dress made her look vulnerable. More approachable than the immaculately dressed secretary he saw more often.

"What can I do for you, Mr. Matheson?" she asked, holding the door like a shield. "Sorry. Dylan."

So much for approachable. "Just wondering how you were feeling. You seemed a little tense downstairs."

"I'm sorry. I felt a little out of place." She looked up at him. "Look. This wasn't a good idea. I should be staying at a hotel like you suggested. I feel like I'm putting your family out."

"You're not at all." Dylan dropped a shoulder against the doorjamb. "Besides, Dara told me that she's bringing some files here tomorrow. Figured it would be easier if we looked at them here, rather than in the office."

Lisa bit her lip, as if considering.

"Look, if it's a problem, we can rent a hotel room. Work out of that."

Lisa shook her head. "No. That's not convenient at all." She glanced up at him. "And for some reason that seems even more compromising than staying here with your parents in the house."

Dylan held her eyes as the faint implications of what she was saying hung between them.

"My dad's at the office and my mother will be running around for the wedding," he said with a light smile.

A spark of awareness arced between them. He let it play out a moment, wondering where it came from. What he was going to do about it.

Lisa lowered her eyes and drew back into the room. "Okay, then. I guess I'll be seeing you tomorrow. What time do you want to start?"

"Eight o'clock okay for you?"

She nodded. "I'll see you then," she said softly, and closed the door.

But Dylan waited, as if trying to analyze that elusive moment.

He would do well to remember Felicia.

And that Lisa was just his secretary.

Chapter Four

Lisa closed the file and rolled the kink out of her neck, easing the tension that had been building the past hour. The stress that pinched her upper shoulders didn't come from her surroundings, however.

Outside the large glass doors behind her, light played through the trees, dancing over the table as classical music played softly through speakers discreetly mounted in the ceiling. The book-lined walls and the two leather couches flanking a fireplace were a temptation she had been ignoring for the past four hours.

Instead the stress came from spending the morning bent over files or staring at a computer screen matching vendors with invoices and getting nowhere close to any thread connected to her brother.

Lisa glanced at Dylan sitting across the table from her. His sleeves were rolled up to just below his elbow, his tie knot hung below his opened collar and his hand was buried in his thick hair. He looked as frustrated as she felt.

As if feeling her scrutiny, he looked up, his disheveled air softening his features. "All done with those?"

"For now. Haven't found anything suspicious, though I'm no accountant."

"You don't need to be an accountant to do what we're doing." Dylan pushed himself away from the table they had set up in the library. " My father just wants us to back up what Dara found about Gabe."

The mention of her brother's name coupled with the irritated tone of Dylan's voice gave Lisa a start.

Lisa took a calming breath. "Why didn't she press charges?"

"My father wouldn't let her. Said he wanted to wait and see how bad the damage really was." Dylan shrugged. "He's a lot more generous than I would have been."

Lisa unconsciously clenched her fists. She said nothing, sure that if she even parted her lips a heated defense of her brother would spill out.

"And now it's time for lunch." Dylan stood. "We'll eat in the kitchen."

Lisa got up and followed him out the door, protesting. "I thought we'd go to a restaurant for lunch." Where she could pay for her own meal and not feel even more indebted to him and his family.

"Why would I want to do that, when all my favorite foods are right here?" Dylan said, and kept walking.

Dylan pulled two plates wrapped in plastic out of

the refrigerator and with a flourish set them on the marble countertop. "Madam, lunch is served."

Each plate held a croissant layered with sprouts, cucumber, tomato and cuts of meat. Tucked beside it was a salad made with multicolored leaves garnished with swirls of carrot and fresh peppers.

"How did you do that?" she asked with mock surprise as he rummaged through a cutlery drawer.

"Secret recipe. A little bit of salt, a sprinkle of cilantro and a whole dose of pleading. My mom made them before she left this morning." Dylan unwrapped the plates and set one on the eating bar in front of her. "Pull up a stool and we'll eat," he said as he tucked the napkin and silverware beside her plate.

Lisa held back. Lunch with just the two of them in the house created an awkward intimacy that wouldn't have happened had they eaten at a restaurant.

"Stop hovering. No one is around. We don't have to pretend right now." Dylan sounded slightly peevish.

Lisa tucked her head down as she pulled up the stool. Were her feelings so transparent? "Sorry, I just feel a little out of place here."

"I gathered that."

She glanced sidelong at Dylan as she unfolded her napkin, taking her cue from him.

He caught her glance and tilted her a half smile. "Don't worry, I'm not the praying type."

"But your family certainly seems to be." Lisa thought back to the supper yesterday. There'd been no awkwardness in the after-supper routine. Every-one had seemed at home with it, even Kerry, Ted and Dara, the guests.

"I used to be." He gave a light shrug as if brush-ing away his past.

"So what happened?"

"Neglect more than anything." He angled his chin toward her. "What about you? You ever go to church?"

She nodded. "When my parents were alive. Yes."

"What made you stop?"

"Their deaths."

Suddenly, to her surprise, she felt Dylan's hand on her arm. But he didn't say anything, and his silence combined with the comforting heaviness of his hand created a surprising bond. His touch was one of sol-ace.

"You still miss them."

"I don't have anyone else." The lie splintered the fragile connection and she pulled away. To cover up, she went on the defensive. "Does your alienation from church have anything to do with your father?"

Dylan sliced through his croissant with one quick movement. "Partly."

"What happened?" Lisa knew she was overstep-ping the boundary between secretary and boss, but she had eaten with his family, was staying in their home. The boundaries were growing blurrier each minute.

Dylan drew in a long, deep breath, then shook his head. "I'm not going to bother you with the details. I was foolish enough to trust that my own father would keep his word.'' He was smiling, but the sharp edge in his voice gave lie to the casual face he was putting on the situation. ''And let's just say Ted has been proving my misgivings correct ever since.''

His ambiguous words made Lisa even more curious. In the short time she'd worked for Dylan she'd sensed he had a steady, solid nature. The kind of man her mother had sought until she found Gabe's father. Dylan's bitterness jarred. Like an off-key note in a harmonious song.

''Is that why you're going to quit?''

''Mostly. I've been waiting too long. It's time I took my life in my own direction.'' He angled his chin at her lunch. ''Now, eat up. We've got a lot of work ahead of us yet before we head out again tonight.''

Lisa caught a flash of yellow through the trees and ran out the door to meet the cab, relief sluicing through her.

Though she had told Dylan she would help him out by being his escort at the wedding, she drew the line at accompanying him to the rehearsal and the rehearsal dinner the family was attending this evening. She desperately wanted to connect with Gabe.

She hopped inside the cab, giving the cabbie Gabe's address, and half an hour after they left Dylan's place, they pulled up in front of a dingy apartment building. Lisa's heart sank. Squat, dark apartment blocks flanked her brother's, and beyond that she saw what looked like the industrial section of Vancouver.

For this she had denied herself countless little luxuries, worked overtime and prayed? So that her brother could end up here?

She pressed the button beside her brother's name, and when she heard his heavy voice answering, she knew he had been sleeping.

As she walked up the stained linoleum of the stairs, she heard the sounds of fighting, a stereo thumping out a deadening bass rhythm.

Home sweet home, she thought, knocking on her brother's door. But in spite of the surroundings, her heart rose with the anticipation of seeing Gabe.

The door opened and Lisa stifled a cry of dismay. Gabe's brown hair lay flat on one side of his head and stuck up on the other. He hadn't shaved. His wrinkled T-shirt and jogging pants looked as if he'd slept in them.

"Hey, Lise," he said, running his fingers through his hair, smiling at her. "Great to see you."

He'd known she was coming, she thought as disappointment flared within her. Surely he could have made some attempt at getting ready?

Then he stepped forward and her arms came up and she was holding her little brother close.

"I missed you, sis," he said giving her a bone-crushing hug.

"I missed you, too." Lisa pulled back, running the palm of her hand over his hair as if to neaten it, love and affection warring with her ever-present desire to improve, to make him better than he was.

"Sorry I look like this. I came off a long shift at work yesterday. Slept most of today." His mouth stretched in a yawn, underscoring his comment. "Come on in. I made you some coffee. Just the way you like it."

Lisa couldn't help scanning the living room as they walked through it, thankful to see that the apartment was reasonably tidy.

"I even have cream," Gabe said, holding aloft a small cardboard container.

"Place looks pretty good, Gabe," Lisa said with forced cheer. She pushed aside a stack of newspapers from the table and sat on the kitchen chair, watching her brother working in the kitchen.

"It's not as nice as my other place was, but hey, we know why I can't afford that anymore. I was lucky enough to find a roommate on such short notice." He handed her a cup of coffee and sat down across the table from her. He smoothed his hair and stifled another yawn. "I can't believe you're actually here in Vancouver."

"I certainly didn't think I'd ever be here this soon." She smiled at Gabe, warmth and love enveloping her. "How's your job?"

Gabe shrugged, stretching his arms out. "It's work and it pays the rent."

"Have you been looking…"

"That's why the stack of newspapers," Gabe said abruptly. "But I can't get a job without a reference and I can hardly use Matheson Telecom. So for now I'm stuck selling telephones and trying to pay bills out of minimum wage." His words spilled out in an angry flow. "I know what you did to help me get this degree. The lousy jobs and the lousy bosses."

He shoved his hands through his hair in a gesture of frustration. "Sorry. I'm just running out of patience."

"It's okay, Gabe. I've got a good job now."

Gabe drew in a deep breath. "And how is it working for Dylan Matheson? Never met the guy, but from the way Dara talks, he was just a cape away from being a superhero."

Lisa had to smile at Gabe's description. "He's an ordinary guy." More ordinary than her first impression of him. "The job is interesting," Lisa said carefully. "I haven't discovered anything helpful. I did meet Dara and Ted."

"Ted kind of stays in the background. Dara's the real power." Gabe leaned back in his chair, balancing it on two legs. Lisa stifled an automatic reprimand. It was his chair. His apartment. "She's a piece of work, isn't she?"

"What do you mean?"

"The whole time I was working for her I got to hear how she wanted to take care of me. She took me out for supper a bunch of times to ask me how I liked my job." He shook his head in disgust. "Things started looking a little shaky and just like that—" he snapped his fingers "—Gabe Haskell is gone and there's no way I can get a reference."

Lisa fingered the handle of the mug. "Did you ever talk to Alex Matheson?"

"Dara wouldn't let me. Told me he wasn't interested." Gabe rocked his chair a moment, pursing his lips.

"Didn't you suspect something was going on?"

"Why do you think I got fired?" Gabe dropped his chair down.

"Are you saying it was a setup?"

Gabe looked at her as if to say, *you silly girl,* and for a moment Lisa felt like the younger of the two, not the other way around.

"If you knew you were right, why didn't you challenge her?" she asked. "Why didn't you go talk to Ted? To Alex?"

"She wouldn't let me. Told me it would make things worse." Gabe pushed himself up from the table and turned away from Lisa, his hands on his hips.

"Gabe, what's going on? What happened there?"

"It's a mess, Lisa. And I don't know how to untangle it." He spun around, caught her by the hands. "You've got to prove me innocent. Without a reference to explain my departure I'll never get a job as an accountant again. Especially in this day and age." He squeezed her hands tighter and tighter as his anger built. "Makes me wonder why I should stay honest."

"Don't you even think about it," Lisa warned, squeezing back. "You've seen what happened to your friends in high school. You've got to do things the right way."

"Much good it's done me so far," he snapped.

"Gabe, please listen to me." Lisa caught his face in her hands, his stubble scratching her palms, and unconsciously she sent up another quick prayer for help. "If you're innocent and Ted or Dara have been the ones fooling with the books, it will come out. I'm working on it now. Me and Dylan. He's smart.

He'll find out the truth." Her own defense of Dylan surprised her. And as she held Gabe's gaze, she could feel the tension flowing out of him.

Thank You, Lord.

The words came from her past, but in spite of a long mistrust of God, she experienced a moment of thankfulness.

"It will come together. I promise."

Gabe's slow smile seemed to seal her declaration. "You're the best sister I could have asked for, you know?" He returned to his chair and sighed lightly. "I haven't prayed for a long time, but I catch myself wondering if I should. Maybe it will help."

"I don't suppose it can hurt."

"Do you still pray, Lisa?"

Lisa thought of her promise to attend church. "Not like I used to."

"I miss it sometimes. But then I think of my dad. Your mom. Us." He shook his head. "It's just you and me, Lisa. You and me against the world."

She nodded at the words they used to encourage each other when it seemed things were conspiring against them. Teachers, social workers, bosses. How many times had she come home from work, dejected and tired, and Gabe had encouraged her and given her the boost she needed? And how often had she done the same for him?

"You and me, buddy. Always and always."

Dylan ran up the walk to the house, whistling a soft tune. The rehearsal and supper had gone better than expected. Though Lisa hadn't attended, her presence in their home, at the supper last night, had all seemed to serve notice to his family that he was, for the moment, taken.

He unlocked the front door of the house and ran up the stairs. But Lisa wasn't in her room. Nor was she in the study or the TV room, or by the swimming pool in the backyard.

She'd said she was going for a walk. Surely she should have been back by now. Had she gotten lost in the woods behind the property?

He was at the back of the house when he heard a vehicle. By the time he walked around past the front Lisa was unlocking the side door. She wore her hair loose this evening, a bounce of curls on her shoulders. The pink shirt and the faded jeans made her look like a cute teenager.

"Hey, there," he said softly so as not to frighten her.

She whirled around, dropping the key. "Where did you come from? I didn't think you'd be back yet." Her words tumbled out in a welter of confusion.

"I ducked out early," he said, puzzled at her reaction. "I thought you would have been back by now."

As Lisa bent to pick up the key, Dylan could see her hand was trembling.

"Are you okay?" he asked.

"Yah. Sure. I'm fine." She laughed lightly. "Just went out for a little while." She handed him the key. "Here."

"Keep it," he said. "You never know when you'll need it again." He looked at her more carefully. Her cheeks were flushed and she wouldn't look him in the eye. Why was she acting so strangely?

"So the rehearsal went okay?" she asked, zipping her purse shut. "No major disasters?"

"We decided to save those for tomorrow," he said with a grin, hoping to put her at ease. He reached past her and opened the door. "Did you want something to drink?"

She shook her head. "I think I'm going to go to bed."

Dylan stifled a beat of disappointment. He had hoped to spend some casual time with her, away from files and computers and his family.

"I imagine you'll want an early start tomorrow?" she asked as they walked toward the stairs.

"I may be a workaholic, but I'm not that bad. Tomorrow this house is going to be a zoo," he said, inwardly shuddering. "Between my sisters, the hairdressers and the photographers, I don't think we'll find a room to work in, let alone some peace and quiet." He stopped at the bottom of the stairs, his hand resting on the metal newel post.

Lisa took one step up, then half turned. "Does that mean my boss is going to let me sleep in?" she asked with a quick grin.

"Go ahead and try. Chelsea is so wound up, she'll be pacing the halls at first light."

"I can imagine she'd be nervous. That's quite a step she's taking."

Dylan held her gaze, wondering. "You ever come close to that?"

"Getting married?" She laughed. "Not a chance.

I've found out the hard way that my stepfather was a rare man. Committed and caring and, even more important, willing to change.'' She grew quiet, her eyes taking on an inward look.

Dylan couldn't let her comment lie, wondering what she meant by it. "You don't think most men are willing to change?"

Lisa gave him a quick sideways look. "No. I think a lot of men are stubborn and proud."

"I know a lot of women who fit that description, as well."

Lisa shrugged his comment off. "I'm sure. But somehow in a man the two emotions seem to be more intense." She angled him a quick smile. "And now that you've received your Lisa lecture, I'm really going to bed."

As Dylan watched her sprint up the stairs, disquiet nudged away the pleasure he had felt just moments ago. And he couldn't help but wonder if she was alluding to the situation between him and his father.

He gave the cold metal of the post a quick tap, as if beating down his thoughts. He doubted she gave his family even a second thought.

Chapter Five

Lisa blotted her lips and tried once more to apply her lipstick. She felt like a stuffed doll, dressed up, fluffed up, perfumed and powdered.

The tangerine-hued dress she had chosen had fit the bill perfectly in the surroundings of the upscale clothing store. Reflected back at her from the mirror of the church's bathroom, it looked flamboyant and overly provocative.

Too late to change it now.

Sucking in her breath, Lisa tossed the matching gauzy scarf over her bare shoulders, smoothed down an errant curl and left the bathroom.

As she entered the foyer the first person who caught her eye was a man in a tuxedo. His broad shoulders were emphasized by the dark cut of the jacket. The white shirt set off the dark color of his hair. He looked stunning.

Lisa's heart flipped once slowly as she recognized Dylan, now transformed.

He wasn't smiling as he came walking toward her, and Lisa's second thoughts about the suitability of her dress crowded back.

"You look amazing," he said softly.

Lisa couldn't think of anything to say in return. Nor could she look away.

"I'm supposed to escort you to your seat," he said, taking her hand.

"I thought that was the usher's job," Lisa said, momentarily bereft of coherent thought.

"Orders of the high command. I'm supposed to make you feel as comfortable as possible." His smile eased some of the tension as he drew her hand through the crook of his arm. The practical part of her told her to pull away, keep her distance. But a small corner of her mind, the empty part that she usually kept a lid on, slowly opened and released a gentle yearning for the closeness he offered.

So she let her hand rest on the stiff material of his coat, let her mind acknowledge the warmth of his arm.

He stopped a moment in the vestibule of the church and Lisa felt her heart flutter again.

The front of the church was a mass of pink Asian lilies and white roses, accented with draped netting. Candles flickered from holders flanking the arrangement. The end of each pew was decorated with swags of chiffon and lilies. Accenting all this splendor was a string quartet, their quiet strains of classical music adding an understated sophistication.

Elegantly expensive.

"I'm guessing I'm supposed to put you on the bride's side of the church," Dylan said, scratching the side of his head in mock puzzlement, unaffected by the display in front of him.

"Seeing as how I know her name and not the groom's, that would be the logical choice." Lisa found her voice and grabbed at her sense of humor to keep her fear at bay. The Matheson home should have been enough to show her how much money they had compared to her and Gabe. This "simple" wedding underscored it.

Dylan led her to an empty spot a few pews back from the front of the church. As she sat down, he leaned over her, a hand on the pew in front of her and beside her. She felt sheltered by his hovering presence.

"Are you going to be okay by yourself?" His gentle half smile nudged her heartbeat up a notch.

To cover up her reaction she flashed him a bright smile and nodded. He waited a moment, as if he was going to say something further. Then he pushed himself away and left.

Lisa forced down a knot of panic, fiddling with the clasp on her purse.

You and me against the world. Gabe's words came back to her, and panic fluttered in her chest once again as she looked around at the perfection that surrounded her. The world she and Gabe were against.

What if Gabe was wrong about these people? What if he *had* stolen the money and she was lying to Dylan's family for nothing?

She had to believe her brother, she thought, clutching the purse with damp hands. Gabe had no reason to lie to her.

Except he had done it before.

Lisa's mouth felt suddenly dry as doubts piled on questions.

Gabe wasn't perfect. Neither was she. And Gabe was all she had. She had to fight for him. For now that meant she had to believe him and she had to stay focused on her plans.

In time the pew beside her filled with other people she didn't know, the women's perfumes blending with the scent of the abundance of flowers in front of the church.

After a while the music changed, a photographer hustled to the front of the church and a rustling through the gathering signaled the beginning of the ceremony.

One of the ushers led the groom's parents down the aisle and sat them down on the other side. After that, Dylan made another entrance, escorting his mother. He sat Stephanie down, his hand resting on her shoulder. He leaned over, talking to her. Stephanie looked up at him, covered his hand with hers and smiled up at her son, her pride evident on her face.

As Dylan turned back, he glanced at Lisa and gave her a quick wink.

It wasn't supposed to mean anything, but combined with the obvious love he had for his mother and his consideration a few moments ago, it created a surge of confusion.

A few moments later a side door near the front of the church opened and the groom, Jordan Strachan, and his attendants filed in, standing in a precise row at the front. Lisa wasn't going to look at Dylan, but it was as if her eyes had their own will and were drawn to his tall figure.

To her consternation, he was looking back at her.

Then the tempo of the music changed again, the congregation shifted and from many of the pews camera bulbs flashed as Amber, the first of the five attendants, came walking down the aisle, wearing a plain navy blue sheath. Silver and cream ribbons were wound around her neck, fluttering far down her back. Simple, thought Lisa, yet formal, setting off to perfection the bouquets of pale pink lilies.

Then, after the last of the attendants were assembled at the front, a hushed murmur flowed through the church, the music swelled and the congregation rose.

Lisa turned to watch Chelsea, now transformed from the bubbly young woman she had met to the classic, blushing bride. Her eyes shone with a happiness that Lisa knew she had never felt. For a moment she felt a clutch of jealousy.

Jordan came forward to take Chelsea from her father, and they exchanged a look that radiated absolute love.

Lisa swallowed down a sudden swelling in her throat, caught up in the purity of their emotions. When she saw Alex kiss his daughter and take his place by his wife she bit her lip to stop its trembling. A storm of odd feelings swirled through her. Even if one were to take away all the exterior trappings of this wedding, Lisa instinctively knew that the happiness and joy she saw now would be as strong in twenty-five years.

Thankfully the minister came to the front and gently put the nervous couple at ease, moving easily from slightly jocular to more serious as he opened his Bible.

''Jordan and Chelsea have chosen Ecclesiastes 4, the second half of verse 12. 'A cord of three strands is not quickly broken.' Knowing Jordan and Chelsea, I find this verse especially appropriate. The two of them have asked to stand before God and His people to be married. Their marriage is not just Jordan and Chelsea, but Jordan, Chelsea and their Lord, whom they love and serve. A powerful cord of three strands.''

As the minister spoke he elaborated on the strength they would receive, as well, from their family. From their community of believers.

The words created a subtle attraction. Gabe's father, Rick, and Lisa's mother, Trish, had enjoyed such a relationship. Their faith had been the cord that bound their family together.

So why had God taken them from her? If God was such a loving God, how did He allow the threefold cord to break?

The memory of her loss jolted her back to reality. She forced herself to think of why she was here. To figure out how she was supposed to exonerate her brother. Lisa turned back to the minister as he wound up his address to the couple, inviting them to speak their vows.

Chelsea's shining eyes, her future husband's stirring words, as he spoke vows they had made up themselves, came across as so authentic and heartfelt.

Though she hardly knew them, Lisa found herself wanting to believe this couple would find their happy ever after. And why not? Lisa thought. Chelsea had a good example in her parents.

Stephanie and Alex had held hands the entire service. Stephanie had brushed away a few tears, and to Lisa's surprise, so had Dylan's father.

Lisa's eyes strayed once more to Dylan. He stood one level below the bridal couple, his hands clasped in front of him, his expression serious as he watched his younger sister pledge her life to her husband.

Dylan was just her boss and a means to an end. But the more she watched him from the safety of the church pew, the more attractive he became. The way he tilted his head down and to the side as he listened. The indentation his mouth created when he smiled his now-familiar half smile. How the light seemed lost in the dark of his hair. He looked even more handsome than the groom, and Lisa couldn't help a stirring of pride in her escort.

At precisely that moment Dylan shifted, caught her eye. Once again their gazes meshed and held, and Lisa felt a faint longing.

"So what God has joined together, let not man put asunder." The preacher's voice boomed out, authority and conviction ringing in the words, echoing in the vastness of the church building. The minister's words yanked Lisa out of the dangerous zone she had slipped into.

Dylan was temporary, she reminded herself, quickly averting her gaze. He needed her and she needed him. Strictly business.

The rest of the service went by in a blur. Lisa could hardly wait until it was over. She couldn't control the ebb and flow of her emotions. From yearning to loss to anger to yearning once again. It was tiring and it had to stop.

Finally the organ started up its joyful celebration music and Chelsea caught the hand of her new husband. With happy smiles and a few waves at people in the audience, they started down the aisle.

And once again Lisa couldn't keep her eyes off Dylan. The crisp white shirt and dark coat were perfect foils for his dark hair and startling gray-blue eyes. He looked like a movie star, she thought as he walked down the aisle. Then he turned, caught her eye, smiled and was gone.

As the family filed out, Lisa was pulled into the wake, Tiffany's husband alongside her. While they walked out, he pointed out various members of the family he seemed to think Dylan's escort should know.

She was part of the family and yet not.

Stop this right now. Lisa clenched her fists, as if squeezing the falsely beguiling thoughts away. She wasn't a part of this and would never be. Especially not if they found out who she really was—the sister of "that accountant."

Thankfully there was no receiving line, and as she

walked out of the church into the warm summer air, she saw Dylan waiting for her.

His smile widened as he caught sight of her.

"There you are," he said softly as he came to her side. "We have to go get pictures taken at the studio. Come with me."

His voice was pitched low, his last three words sounding like an intimate invitation. Lisa didn't want to read more into them than mere convenience, but the peculiar feeling that had gripped her in church would not be dispelled.

"Surely I don't need to come?"

Dylan shrugged, shook his head, his eyes holding hers. "It would just make things easier. After that we go straight to the reception, so you may as well come with me."

Lisa nodded, forcing herself to look away from his mesmerizing gaze. It was the startling contrast of those gray-blue eyes and dark eyebrows and hair that always caught her attention. Like a puzzling surprise that needed further investigation to figure out.

Not because she was falling for him. Not at all.

The twins had found a ride with a friend, so Dylan and Lisa rode by themselves to the photography studio. Lisa kept thinking of the ceremony she had just witnessed. Dylan was quietly whistling one of the songs from the service.

Being Dylan's escort had seemed so simple back in Toronto. It had been easier to think of this all in the abstract rather than the concrete. In her life she had much experience with coming and going into other families, so she'd thought this would be much the same.

Until she'd seen Dylan greeted with a hug from his mother. Until she'd sat through a church wedding that was more than just a tradition, more than an idle gesture. Sincere prayers had been spoken, heartfelt songs had been sung. In spite of Dylan's distance from his father, she saw a love for God that spanned generations. Grandparents from both sides of each family were there. Aunts, uncles and cousins.

This was a family with a history of togetherness and faith.

"You're pretty quiet," Dylan said finally as they followed the limousine into the parking lot of the photography studio.

"Tired, I think," she said, unable to look at him. She felt as if she had put herself out on a limb, first taking on the job, then meeting his family. Each move, each event pushed her further and further out to a world she had to negotiate with care. If they knew about Gabe...

And she had a whole week to get through yet.

It's just a game, she thought. Just play it through till the end.

She was about to get out of the car when Dylan caught her arm.

"Lisa, just a minute," he said, his voice quiet.

With a frown she turned to him, wondering what he might want to say.

"I want to thank you for doing this for me. You really have no idea what you've saved me from."

He smiled, and Lisa felt again that unwelcome nudge of attraction.

"Not a problem, Dylan." She glanced at him, affecting a breezy air. "I got a taste of what you were in for the other night at suppertime."

Dylan angled his head to one side, as if studying her. "I also want to thank you for all the extra time you've put in."

"I'm not phoning the labor relations board yet."

Dylan laughed. "I wish I had your ability to turn things into a joke." He leaned back against his window, as if settling in for a heart-to-heart chat.

Something Lisa didn't have the defenses for now. "You know the saying 'Laugh and the world laughs with you. Cry and you'll end up on an afternoon talk show.'" She winked at him, hoping she could keep this up.

"You've got this tough exterior," he said. "Yet I get a feeling that's due to hurt layered beneath."

Lisa's heart wanted to believe that what she would say mattered to him. Her yearnings for family had often included someone exactly like Dylan. But she knew the reality of the situation. She needed him to find out the truth about her brother. She couldn't afford to let him into her life. Couldn't open the tiniest crack to him.

Yet, yet…

"Everyone has some hurt in their life," she conceded quietly, giving him the few crumbs she dared. Then she dared a little more. "I know you have."

Dylan rubbed the bridge of his nose and sighed. "What do you mean?"

Lisa had gotten too far to quit now. "Your father. You. Ted. Today I saw a family that has solidity. Harmony. Except for a few harsh notes."

He turned back to her and gave her a careful smile. "And you care because…?" He angled his head to one side.

"Because I don't have a family," she said quietly, her defenses worn down by the ceremony she had just witnessed. By Dylan's nearness. "Because I would give all I have for even a small part of what you have in your family."

"That's important to you?"

"What is rare becomes precious." Lisa stopped the words flowing out of the lonely place.

"I think people in your life have let you down, too." He caught her hand, tugging on it.

She couldn't allow this to happen, she warned herself. She couldn't start allowing him in. Because what would she have when they went their separate ways? What she had before. Only Gabe.

"Actually, there have been a lot of people in my life. A superb and varied cast." She pulled away from him with a light laugh. "Too bad I haven't quite figured out the plot." With a twist of her wrist she had the door open and she was outside. Two quick breaths and equilibrium was restored.

She closed her eyes, pressed her lips together as she pulled into herself and the secret place she retreated to when her life was being taken apart by psychiatrists and social workers.

Take care of yourself. Take care of Gabe, she repeated as she mentally wrapped her layers of protection around herself.

You and me against the world.

The photographs took longer than the hour Dylan had promised and Lisa had to endure the subtle torment of seeing Dylan under selected lighting posing with his family, his sister. With each flash of the photographer's bulb, each new pose, she found herself watching him more and more.

It's just the tuxedo, she thought. It gave him a distinguished air that showed her a man who was at ease with himself no matter the circumstances. A man who could smile away the teasing of his family, who could give as good as he got without any rancor or anger.

Finally the last pose was held, the last photo snapped. Lisa slipped on her sandals and stood, brushing her dress down in anticipation of leaving.

"Wait a minute." Chelsea motioned to Lisa and her heart sank. Surely Chelsea didn't want her in the family picture? "I think Dylan and Lisa should get their picture taken. We've never had one of Dylan and a girlfriend." Chelsea caught Dylan by the arm, bringing him to the center of the studio with a swish of her taffeta dress. "C'mon, Lisa."

Lisa held back, her eyes darting to Dylan, pleading with him silently. They couldn't do this. It was a farce.

Dylan tried to talk his way out of it, but soon the other sisters joined the chorus. He turned to Lisa and with a shrug held out his hand to her.

She had no choice but to join him.

"That looks great," the photographer enthused. "The colors of that dress with the tux. Superb." He walked over to them and pushed them closer together. "Put your hand on her shoulder, the other on her waist." Dylan obliged and Lisa fought the urge to push it off. She felt exposed, standing here with him in the circle of light, surrounded by his family.

"Okay…Lisa, is it?"

Lisa felt Dylan's hand squeeze her shoulder and she looked up, realizing she hadn't paid attention.

"Lisa, put your opposite hand on Dylan's hand at your waist. Now lean back, just a bit. Dylan, you come forward."

Lisa could feel Dylan's breath teasing the hair at her temple, could feel the heaviness of his hands on her shoulder and waist.

"Smile for the camera, Lisa," Dylan whispered in her ear.

"This is silly," she whispered back.

"Just play along," he replied, the hand at her waist squeezing her lightly. "We don't need to keep the pictures." He caught her fingers through his and pulled her ever so gently closer.

"That's great," the photographer said. "Just great."

Lights flashed and Lisa started.

"Just a couple more." More flashes.

They were posed again, this time face-to-face.

"Look at each other with a big smile," they were encouraged.

Lisa didn't want to look up into his eyes again.

Didn't want to feel herself slowly being drawn into his personality, himself.

Love at first sight was only for fairy tales and people who couldn't think for themselves.

Everything is just a game, she reminded herself as she lifted her chin. And you know the rules. She had to act like a loving escort. Had to treat him as if he was special. He was technically her boss, after all.

But as Dylan looked down at her, she found herself wondering how she was going to manage to treat this whole thing like a game for six more days.

Dylan took a quick gulp of punch, looking around at the hall where the reception was being held. Fountains and gorgeous tall centerpieces, flowers and netting decorated the elegant room. All around him people laughed and joked. In the middle of the dance floor couples moved to the rhythm of the music.

He'd done his duty dance with the bridesmaid, his sisters, his mother and a few aunts. He'd caught up with some uncles and a few cousins who had waylaid him a couple of times.

And thanks to his duties, he still hadn't had a chance to dance with Lisa. She was supposed to be with him, yet it seemed that she had danced with everyone but him.

As Dylan watched, the young man she was dancing with caught her hand and pulled her close to tell her something. Lisa listened, then pulled back, laughing.

Dylan knew he had nothing to be jealous of. Lisa was just here for his convenience. He would be foolish to deny Lisa a good time, but he didn't think she needed to be having that much fun.

Especially when he didn't feel as if he was. Her words in the car about his family had found a home. He knew he had to fix what was wrong in his relationships, but how could he when his misgivings about Ted had been proven beyond a doubt? The fact that he was here trying to untangle the mess created under Ted's leadership should prove to his father conclusively that he had made a mistake.

Yet Alex said nothing. Did nothing.

And spending this much time with his family underscored the distance between him and his father. He was surrounded by family and friends, yet he felt completely alone.

He didn't have to be. Amber and Erika had been wonderfully prudent, though they had each taken along a couple of friends. Not once in the course of the evening, however, had they approached him or introduced him to any of their girlfriends. Not once had he been forced to dance with a giddy young girl whose breathless conversation was sprinkled with *like*s and *you know*s.

Lisa's presence was doing exactly what he had hoped it would. The wedding he had been dreading was turning out just fine. So why wasn't he feeling happier?

"Hey, Dylan." His father's brother, Anton Matheson, caught him by the arm, turning him around. "How are you, boy?"

Dylan grinned at his uncle and allowed himself to be drawn into a hearty hug. Anton was shorter than

Dylan by a head, but he exuded a force of will that made him seem a foot taller. Anton pulled away, his dark eyes piercing Dylan's. "So how are you really?"

The shift in his uncle's tone moved the conversation from a casual give-and-take to the shakier territory of emotions.

"It was a lovely ceremony."

Anton nodded, the overhead lights glinting off his shiny forehead. "I heard you're quitting. Leaving the company?"

"It's time to move on. I'm not going anywhere."

Anton's slow smile disappeared into the wiry brush of his mustache. "I'm sorry to hear that. I'm sure your father is even more so."

Annoyance twitched through him. "Truthfully, Uncle Anton, I think this makes things a whole lot easier for my father. He can keep Ted in charge without any guilt."

"I think your father is struggling with his own regrets."

Dylan tugged at his tie, feeling suddenly restricted by it. "I wouldn't know. I haven't heard much from him."

Anton nodded, brushing his index finger over his mustache. "Pride is a strong Matheson trait. You might have to make the first move."

"I have." Dylan tossed down the last of his punch, stifling his annoyance. His uncle didn't need to be treated to a display of family disunity.

Anton caught Dylan's angry gaze, a soft smile

playing around his lips. "Your father does care about you."

Dylan put his cup down and leaned forward. "Uncle Anton, I really appreciate that you're trying to do this, but I've given all I can as far as my father is concerned. I've come to help the company. Not him. And if my father is really concerned about our relationship, then I would say it's up to him to do something about it."

Dylan felt the anger leave him as he spoke.

Anton nodded. "I know what you're saying, Dylan. And you're right. Now let's talk about something pleasant. Maybe that lovely young woman you're with. Tell me some more about her."

Dylan glanced at the dance floor where Lisa was laughing at something her partner was saying.

"Her name is Lisa."

Anton nodded, and Dylan could almost hear his smirk.

"She's beautiful."

Dylan didn't have to echo that remark. But it made him uncomfortable to talk to his dear uncle about a relationship that was strictly for convenience.

It made him feel guilty. As if he was using Lisa.

Lisa and the man on the dance floor made another twirl, and thankfully the music came to an end.

"Well, here's my chance to dance with her, Uncle Anton. I'll catch you later."

Anton waved him off. "Go. Enjoy yourself."

Couples drifted off the dance floor as Dylan walked toward Lisa. With a surge of relief Dylan watched as Lisa shook her head, obviously declining another dance. Then, turning, she walked straight to him.

"Did you have a good time?"

"I've had more fun at the dentist," she muttered, keeping her smile intact.

Dylan couldn't help but laugh, surprised at the relief he felt at her annoyance. "He couldn't have been that bad—you danced two dances with him."

"He didn't understand the meaning of the word *no*." Lisa shook her head. "Maybe he's dyslexic."

"He's my cousin."

Lisa stopped, looked away and then back at him with a shrug. "Sorry. I didn't know."

"Can't pick your relatives."

"Oh, the joys of splashing in the gene pool."

Dylan laughed out loud as pleasure spiraled up in him, replacing his earlier melancholy.

The music changed tempo, the lights dimmed and Dylan glanced at the dance floor. Couples were moving closer together. In the middle he saw his sister Chelsea with her new husband, her arms clasped around his neck. He saw his parents, Tiffany and her husband.

Everyone paired up. Belonging to someone.

"Can I have this dance?" he asked, looking back at Lisa.

"I'm not very good at slow dances," she said with a light laugh.

"It's not hard. Just follow my lead."

"I'm not much good at doing that, either."

"Try," Dylan urged. He caught her hand and took

a step toward the dance floor, smiling encouragement at Lisa.

With a laugh she finally gave in. Then they were on the floor, facing each other.

"Do we have to pretend to be a devoted couple?" Lisa asked with a touch of irony in her voice.

"No, but you can pretend you're having a good time." Dylan pushed down his disappointment at her response. He caught her hand in his, slipped his arm around her waist.

"I don't know if I can rise to the occasion," she said, flashing him a teasing grin. "But I can slide over to it."

"Then you'd be dancing," he replied, laughing, thankful once again for the equilibrium her sense of humor created.

However, when he pulled her closer, Dylan drew in a slow breath, feeling a release from the tension of the past few hours.

It was like coming home, he thought, turning slowly in time to the music. As if everything crazy in his life suddenly made sense with Lisa in his arms.

It was ridiculous to think that a girl he had just met could mean anything to him. And, even more, she was his employee. He blamed his feelings on the corny sentiments that single people often felt at weddings.

But the litany of practical phrases couldn't explain the absolute rightness of having her in his arms.

He held her, beguiled by her touch, the faint scent of the shampoo in her hair. She wore no perfume, no other fragrance, yet he caught the fragile scent that he now recognized as peculiar to Lisa.

All too soon the dance was over, the lights came up and the moment drifted away with the last haunting notes of the music. Lisa didn't look up at him as she slowly straightened. Her fingers trailed down the lapels of his coat. Had she felt it, too?

Dylan wanted to say something, to deepen the connection they had just experienced.

Then, finally, she glanced up at him, her eyes sparkling with mischief. "Don't look so somber, Dylan. Life is too serious to be taken seriously." She tapped her fingers on his chest, then pulled away. Dylan scowled at her, disappointment spiraling tightly through him. How could she so casually dismiss what had just happened? Hadn't she felt it, as well?

"I'm going to freshen up my lipstick," she said, taking a step back. "Thanks for the dance."

As she turned and walked away, annoyance twisted through him. Lately little satisfied him anymore.

Chapter Six

A sliver of light played across Lisa's eyelids, pulling her out of the half-sleeping state she had drifted in and out of for the past hour.

She glanced at the clock beside her bed. Six-thirty.

She wouldn't be able to sleep anymore, even though fatigue still pressed down on her. The party last night hadn't wound down until three-thirty. Then she had stayed with the rest of the family, cleaning up what they could and loading up the presents in the van hired for the purpose.

She was still tired, but hoped to spend some time this morning without Dylan around. Hoped to ease the jangling in her nerves that had started last night when Dylan had held her in his arms. She had tried to rationalize her reaction, but couldn't get past the part of her that had responded to him.

Thankfully the bathroom was unoccupied, so she had a quick shower. She slipped on a pair of loose-fitting pants and topped it with a T-shirt. Dylan had declared that they would take the morning off, but she hoped to get in a few undisturbed hours of work in spite of that. It would remind her why she was here.

She crept down the carpeted stairs, pausing a moment outside the study. The lonely echo of a dripping kitchen tap was the only sound to break the utter stillness of a house asleep. She felt like a burglar.

Suppressing a shiver of guilt, Lisa let herself into the study. In a matter of moments she had the computer booted up and the files she needed laid out on the table. She glanced at her careful notes to get herself up to speed and started the methodical work she had begun before the wedding.

In spite of the emotional investment she had tied up in this work, she found a peculiar serenity in the tediousness of the matching process, and soon her agitated spirits were soothed.

The muted bonging of the grandfather clock in the corner marked off the hour. Startled, Lisa looked up at the time. Eight o'clock and still no sounds drifted down from the bedrooms upstairs.

Lisa rolled her shoulders, and as she looked around the room she gave in to the lure of the bookshelves crammed full. Just a moment, she promised herself. A break.

But as her fingers trailed along the spines of the novels, she felt the pull of familiar titles—classics and modern novels that had at one time granted her solace either from the tedium of a boring job or the stress of the responsibility of raising Gabe.

She moved along and was confronted by a section of nonfiction books. And from the sounds of the titles, all of them Christian books.

Books by theologians jostled modern books promising help and guidance for life's various circumstances.

A Bible lay on its side on one of the shelves and Lisa picked it up. To put it away, she told herself. But she couldn't find an empty space for it.

So she held it, her fingers lightly tracing the embossing on the cover. She flipped it open and glanced down the pages, the familiar words drawing up memories from another period in her life.

Lisa ran her finger down the pages as if touching the words made them more real. She knew the patterns and rhythms. Once they had been a part of her life; once they had given her comfort. She started reading.

"'How lovely is Your dwelling place....'" She whispered the words of Psalm eighty-four, the phrases part of a life left behind when she and Gabe had walked away from the graveyard as orphans.

But the words created a yearning she had long suppressed. "'Better is one day in Your courts than a thousand elsewhere.'" The language was dated, but it dived deep into her heart. And she remembered the promise she had made when she'd prayed her foolish prayer in Dylan's office. To attend church.

"Excuse me."

The voice at the door scattered the emotions of the moment and she slapped the Bible shut, laying it on the shelf in front of her.

She turned to face Dylan's father as he entered the study, her heart fluttering with guilt. "I'm sorry. I didn't mean to intrude."

"Don't apologize." Alex smiled carefully at her and lowered himself into one of the leather chairs flanking the fireplace. "Our home is yours as long as you are here." He indicated the sofa diagonally across from him. "Sit down a moment." Alex let his head drop against the back of the chair, but kept his eyes on Lisa. "Are you enjoying your stay here?"

She nodded as she sank into the soft leather of the couch, once again aware of the kindly warmth this man exuded.

"You and Dylan…" He paused, then smiled at her. "How long have you been dating?"

Lisa held Alex's gaze, her emotions in turmoil. Though this man had been involved in what had happened with her brother, she remembered his warm welcome. The connection she felt with him that she couldn't simply pass off. She was surprised no one had asked the question sooner. But the ruse she and Dylan were playing was Dylan's secret to keep and to divulge.

"Our relationship has been somewhat ephemeral," she said, the vagueness of her words making her wince inwardly. Nerves always brought out the long words.

"I see." Alex nodded, a smile playing around lips identical in shape to those of his son's. "In spite of that, Dylan seemed quite attentive to you when you were dancing."

Lisa couldn't stop the flush that warmed her

cheeks. She chose silence as her answer. Anything she said would either accuse her or make her look as if she was making excuses.

"You'll have to excuse my bluntness," Alex said, his fingers doing a light dance on the armrest of his chair. "Though we've just met, I have a good feeling about you. You're the first girlfriend of Dylan's that the family has ever met."

Lisa felt even more of a fraud.

"I guess what I'm trying in my clumsy way to say is, I still hope he'll find someone good," he continued. "That one of my boys will make good choices." His voice seemed tinged with regret.

Lisa assumed he referred to Ted and wondered what his vague comment meant.

"I've only known Dylan a few weeks, but I think you can trust him to do that," she said quietly.

Alex raised his head at her defense of his son, his eyes lighting up. "Dylan is a man of principle and values. I haven't always been fair with him."

Lisa thought of how Dylan's voice grew harsh whenever he talked about Alex. She shouldn't care what happened between them.

But as she looked at Alex she couldn't help but remember how he and his wife had held hands during their daughter's wedding. How he had glanced at his wife a few times with such obvious love in his eyes.

"But you are a good father," she said softly. "And Dylan can be thankful for such good parents."

"I understand your parents are dead. I'm sorry to hear that."

"They died a while ago. I was fifteen."

"So young. How did you manage?"

"I was always kind of independent." In spite of her casual words, she felt a warm glow at his concern. What she wouldn't have given for even a scrap of what Dylan had with his family.

"I sensed you were a woman of strength. But I want you to know that as long as you and Dylan are together, this family is yours, too."

Lisa held his gaze, and to her surprise she felt her eyes tear up. Alex had given her more than a scrap. He had given her everything he had.

She looked away, unable to speak.

As if sensing her discomfort Alex pushed himself away from the chair and walked over to the table. "Have you and Dylan made any headway on this problem?"

His tact gave her a chance to quickly wipe away the moisture from her eyes. "It's too early yet," she said, thankful that she sounded more composed than she felt. "All we've been doing is matching invoices to vendors...." Her voice trailed off as she hesitated over her next suggestion. "What I really think you need to do is hire an external auditor to take care of this."

Alex waved off her suggestion, then picked up a file and thumbed through it. "Maybe later. But right now I prefer to keep this internal until we find out for sure what that accountant has done."

"That accountant" happened to be her brother. The words were a chilling reminder of where she secretly stood in this family.

On the opposite side.

A sudden edginess propelled her off the couch. "If you'll excuse me, I'm going to go back to my room," she said.

Alex glanced up at her, smiling again as if he hadn't heard the tight tone of her voice. "Breakfast is very casual this morning. Our housekeeper put a few things out on the buffet in the dining room, so please help yourself."

"Thank you."

"I should let you know, as well, that most of the family will be leaving for church at about ten-thirty. Just so you don't think we're deserting you."

Lisa felt a jolt of disappointment that he automatically assumed she would be staying behind. At one time she would have gone. Her eyes slid past him to the Bible on the shelf.

Whatever your lips utter you must be sure to do.

"I was wondering..." She drew in a shaky breath, then plunged ahead. "I was wondering if it would be possible to come along?"

Alex's head snapped up. Then with a half smile reminiscent of Dylan's he nodded. "That would be wonderful. We'll let you know half an hour before we leave."

She returned his smile, then walked out of the study. But a sudden restlessness made her turn toward the dining room instead of up to her bedroom.

As promised, the buffet along the wall held a glass-covered plate of assorted muffins, a carafe of coffee, plates of fruit. She was still alone, so Lisa took her plate of food out onto the deck. Wicker chairs were pulled up to a glass table; Lisa sat down in one of them.

A soft breeze sifted up the hill, swishing through the fir trees bordering the property. Below her, softened by the early-morning haze, lay the inlet and the city of Vancouver. Lisa couldn't help a wry smile as she buttered her muffin. You fraud, she thought, taking a bite. Acting as if this is so natural.

Only a week ago she had been sitting on a completely different balcony, staring directly at the apartment block only a few meters across the alley from hers, also eating a muffin. Only, hers was plain bran, picked up from the day-old bakery section of the convenience store close to her apartment.

This one had a hint of mango and spices she couldn't identify. Gourmet muffin, she thought, taking another pleasurable bite, eaten on the balcony of a gourmet home.

''So, here's where you're hiding.''

Lisa spun around, almost upsetting the plate on her lap.

Dylan stood behind her, shoulders hunched, his hands in the pockets of his blue jeans. His shirt was unbuttoned, revealing a T-shirt underneath. His feet were bare.

Lisa felt her heart do a slow flip, his casual dress affecting her just as much as his formal dress of yesterday had.

''You've finally decided to get up?'' she asked, covering her reaction to him by turning back to her breakfast.

''Finally? I've only gotten about five hours'

sleep.'' He pushed himself away from the wall and walked over to the table. "How's the food?"

"Superlative."

"Most people would just say good," he said with a grin. He dropped into the chair across from her, propping his ankle on his knee as he massaged his neck. His hair was still damp from his shower. "What are your plans?"

Lisa wiped her mouth, wondering what his reaction would be. "I'm going to church with your family."

Dylan did a double take. "Church? Why?"

Lisa felt suddenly self-conscious. "I used to when I was younger."

"Do you feel you need to confess something?" Dylan asked, slanting her a playful grin.

He's just joking, Lisa reminded herself, pushing down the flare of shame his words kindled in her. "I just feel like attending church," she said, setting her knife across her plate. She couldn't eat any more.

"That would leave me on my own." Dylan almost pouted. "I guess I'll have to come along."

"Surely you don't have to keep up this devoted couple thing?" Lisa protested. Spending every waking moment with him was making it too hard to maintain her professional distance.

Dylan shrugged and picked up an uneaten strawberry from her plate. "Maybe I want to go, too?" he said, popping the strawberry into his mouth.

"I can hardly stop you." She stood up, brushing the few wayward crumbs from her pants, and picked up her plate.

''Wait a minute.'' He caught her lightly by the wrist and took the other strawberry from her plate.

''Why don't you get your own?'' she said with a nervous laugh. His fingers were warm. If it hadn't been for the plate she held so precariously, she would have pulled her hand back.

''Not that hungry,'' he said, licking his fingers. He looked up at her, his hand still shackling her wrist. ''Did you have a good time last night?''

She nodded and gently reclaimed her arm. ''You have a wonderful family.'' It was easier to talk about his family than the dance they'd shared. Or how for the rest of the night whenever they were apart her eyes had found and followed him. ''I had a nice chat with your father in the study this morning.''

''Did you, now.'' Dylan squinted up at her, rocking lightly in his chair.

Lisa thought of the pain she saw on Alex's face each time Dylan turned away from him. ''I like your father, Dylan.''

Dylan's laugh was without humor. ''And I think he likes you. Too bad you're just my secretary.''

It was the truth and it shouldn't have hurt. But it did.

''I better get ready,'' she said softly, turning away. To her dismay, however, Dylan followed her.

One of the twins sat at the table, hunched over a section of the newspaper, eating a bagel. She was wrapped in a fuzzy bathrobe, her wet hair slicked back from her face.

''Hey, Amber,'' Dylan said, tousling her hair. ''Get all the hair spray out?''

Amber tilted her head backward to look up at her brother. "Barely. What about you?"

Dylan gave her hair a light tug. "I don't use that girly stuff."

"Really? Then why is most of Erika's pomade gone?" She turned around, grinning at him. "She said you borrowed it."

Dylan just shrugged off her comment and pulled up a chair. Amber glanced at Lisa, her smile growing. "Not only that, he used my blow-dryer. I think he was just trying to impress you, Lisa. Dylan hardly ever fusses with his hair."

Lisa didn't think the comment required a response, and Dylan was paging through the newspaper, patently ignoring his little sister.

"I'm going to get ready," Lisa said.

Amber frowned up at Lisa. "Ready for what?"

"I'm coming to church with you and your family. If that's okay."

Amber scratched her cheek with her forefinger, looking disheartened. "Yeah. I guess."

"If it's a problem…"

"No, that's not it. It was just that Erika and I…" She flipped her hand Lisa's way. "Never mind."

"It's just you had plans?" Dylan asked without looking up. "Inviting someone to come along, perhaps?"

Amber's blush verified Dylan's comment, and Lisa stifled a laugh. A person had to give the girls marks for persistence.

"I'll be ready in a while, Dylan," Lisa said, her

hand brushing his shoulder in a subtle proprietary motion. A silent signal to Amber.

Now Dylan looked up. Then he smiled as he realized what she was doing. ''I'll be waiting,'' he said, catching her hand. He squeezed it, and when Lisa tried to pull it back he held it for just a split second longer, then let her go.

Lisa felt her cheeks grow warm, and she regretted her impulse. But by the time she was back in her room, her heartbeat had returned to normal.

She pulled out a cheerfully embroidered peasant blouse and a denim skirt, hoping they were suitable for church. Neither her mother nor Rick had fussed much about clothes when they'd attended, but had emphasized respect and modesty in their choice of clothing.

As Lisa styled her hair, she thought of those Sunday mornings. Remembered the gentle chaos of getting four people to one place at the same time, neatly dressed and clean. Then the church service and the feeling of reverence and awe blended with the presence of God's love that came from worshiping with fellow believers.

It was a wonderful time of her life. Something she wanted for herself and her children.

Something that Dylan's family had.

Cued by the minister, Dylan and the rest of the congregation sat down. As Dylan sat, he took another quick glance at Lisa, who was still clutching the hymnal they had just sung from. Her head was bent and her hair, worn loose this morning, hid her face. She seemed to be intently reading from the hymnal.

When she had told him this morning that she wanted to go to church, he couldn't have been more surprised than if she had asked to go to a bar. Granted, he didn't know her that well, but he'd assumed that church and faith were not important to her.

They weren't important to him, either. As he had told Lisa, it wasn't anything big and dramatic that had caused his slide away from faith and church. Moving to Toronto, away from his family, had been the first step. Working six days a week to prove himself had been the second. Sunday had been his only day off, and he'd started resenting getting up early to go to church. He'd begun to date girls who had nothing to do with church and zero interest in matters of faith. And slowly his church attendance had eased off to nothing.

He used to feel guilty on the Sunday mornings he was up early for the occasional meeting or a flight out of town, but that had passed, as well.

It was sad how easy it had been to drift away, he thought. Now that he was here, he was sorry he had cut out this part of his life.

Dylan pulled the Bible out of the rack and turned to the passage announced by the minister.

"'How lovely is Your dwelling place, O Lord almighty. Better is one day in Your courts than a thousand elsewhere.'"

To his surprise, Dylan felt a throb of guilt, edged with sorrow. He had missed all this, he thought, following the words with his index finger as the minister read them. The words drew back old memories—of happier times when he and his brother were friends, not enemies. When they were both unaware of the words *favoritism, injustice.* When they weren't in competition for their father's affection.

Dylan read on, allowing the words to gently dislodge memories of better times.

And how could they go back to that?

He was quitting the company to strike out on his own. Under Ted's guidance the company that his father had started and was hoping to ease away from was starting to unravel.

And he and his father and his brother spoke to each other only when necessary.

He closed the Bible before the minister finished reading and slipped it back in the holder with a hollow *thunk.* He didn't want to read about family unity and respect anymore. Right now he didn't have a lot of respect for his father and his lack of backbone. And his frustration with his brother hardly promoted family unity.

He was actually thankful to his father right now for asking him to come and help figure out what had happened to the company. Up until now he'd been still having second thoughts about leaving Matheson Telecom.

He didn't anymore.

But even as resentment sifted through him, he couldn't help but listen to the minister's words. He spoke of the yearning God had to be closer to His people. How God wanted us to be yearning for Him. In spite of his resistance, Dylan felt the words push against the walls of anger and bitterness he had erected against his father and brother. He felt as if he hardly dared let God's love breach that. Because then what reason would he have to keep going down the road he had taken?

When the minister announced the song after the sermon, he was still thinking, wondering.

Lisa pulled the hymnal out of the rack and opened it up. As the organ played a short introduction to the song, she lowered her head. He saw her swipe at her cheek, heard a faint sniff.

She dug in her purse and pulled out a tissue. As she wiped her nose, she angled her head. Dylan was shocked to see the glistening track of tears on her cheeks. But before he could say or do anything, she was looking down again.

He glanced down at the hymnal on her lap, reading the first few lines of the song.

"The tender love a father has for all his children dear…"

The words drew out a mixture of emotions. Dylan had a father who preferred one son over the other.

Lisa had no father at all.

For a moment sorrow replaced Dylan's anger, and it was that shared sorrow that made him slip his arm around her shoulders. Draw her to his side.

Her slight resistance was followed by a gentle drifting toward him, and he pulled her closer. And

once again he felt that same connection that had
sparked between them last night.

That it had happened in church seemed to add a
blessing to the moment.

Pull yourself together, Lisa commanded herself,
bending over the sink of her bedroom's en suite. She
splashed cold water on her puffy eyes, wiped her
running mascara and drew in a deep breath.

She didn't have to feel guilty anymore. Her obligation had been fulfilled. She had gone to church just
as she had promised.

So why did she feel as if her carefully constructed
life was unraveling piece by piece?

The moment in church when she had so clearly
felt the call of God to come to Him and let Him be
a father to her still brought tears to her eyes. And
she hardly ever cried.

Almost as precious was the memory of Dylan putting his arm around her. A pang of yearning sang
through her, agitating a flurry of emotions she never
thought she'd feel again.

Dylan is leaving and you are living a lie.

That cold reality sobered her more than the water
had.

She left the sanctuary of her bedroom to join the
family outside.

And of course the first person she saw when she
stepped through the large glass doors to the deck was
Dylan. He stood in profile to her, talking with his
mother. As he smiled she felt the advent of her previous feelings and she quickly looked away, frustrated at how quickly they had returned.

"Lisa, can I get you anything to drink?" Alex was beside her, smiling down at her.

"No. Thanks."

"And how did you enjoy church?" he asked, drawing her aside.

Lisa glanced up at him, at the features so like his son's, except softened by age. "I'm glad I went," she said, glad she could be honest about something. "It was a real blessing."

Alex's smile blossomed. "I'm so glad to hear that."

"Dad, here's your iced tea." Ted joined them then, handing his father a tall frosted glass. "Well, hello, Lisa. Where have you been hiding? I stopped by an hour ago, but neither you nor my brother were home."

"Dylan and Lisa came to church with us," Alex said quietly, a faint edge to his voice.

Ted's eyebrows shot up and he quirked her a wry grin. "Dylan? In church? You are a surprising influence on my brother, Lisa. I guess there's hope for him after all."

"Well, false hope is better than no hope at all," Lisa quipped.

"So have you and Dylan been able to corroborate what Dara has discovered?" Ted asked her. "I know she's been quite upset about the whole problem. Quite disturbing."

Lisa nodded, wishing she'd taken Alex up on his offer of something to drink. She might have missed talking to Ted. There was a hollow heartiness about him that rang false. As if he was trying too hard to be who he was. She never felt comfortable around him.

"Nothing that's jumped out at us yet." She angled him a quick glance. "Maybe he didn't do it."

Ted laughed. "Oh, he did it, all right." Ted turned to his father. "I still don't know why you're bothering with this. It's over. We found out who did it. Let's carry on."

Alex swirled his iced tea in his glass and shook his head. "It's not over yet, Ted. I want to be sure beyond any reasonable doubt that we have done the right thing."

Ted bit his lip and jerked his head to one side, as if holding back some retort.

"What's not over yet?" Dylan asked, coming to stand beside Lisa.

She kept her eyes on Alex, but every fiber of her being was aware of Dylan behind her. She caught the faint scent of his aftershave, then almost started when he laid a light hand on her shoulder. Part of the act, she reminded herself, suppressing another shiver.

"Your make-work project," Ted said with a sigh. He gave his brother a quick glance. "The job Dad dragged you back here to do in the hopes that he could talk you into staying with Matheson Telecom."

Lisa felt Dylan's fingers tighten on her shoulder, but his voice betrayed no emotion at all. "That won't happen, Ted. But I'm glad to help out while I'm here."

''Trust me, Dylan. It's a setup. There's nothing to do here.'' Then he turned and left them.

Dylan released the pressure on Lisa's shoulder, but didn't remove his hand. ''Is that true, Dad? Was my coming here just a ruse?''

Alex's gaze was steadfast, his smile tinged with regret. But he shook his head. ''No, Dylan. I truly need your help in this matter.''

''You know my abilities are limited. So are my resources. If you are serious about this, you'll hire an outside auditor.''

''Trust me on this son. Not yet.''

''Trust.'' The word exploded above her head, and Lisa almost flinched at the anger in it. ''May I remind you that it was trusting you that got us into this mess, Dad.''

Alex winced, then nodded. ''You're right, son.''

Lisa chanced a quick glance up at Dylan. His jaw was set, his eyes narrowed.

She felt caught up in a storm of feelings, yet felt as if they were on the verge of something big. Important.

The moment stretched between them, then Alex turned away.

Dylan's hand slipped off her shoulder and he drew it over his face. ''I need to get out of here,'' he said, glancing down at her. ''You want to come for a drive?''

She looked back over her shoulder at Alex, who now stood beside his wife. She wanted to run after him. Pull him back. Make him face his son's anger and deal with it.

For Dylan's sake and his own.

But Dylan was supposed to be her boyfriend, and until he told her different, she was to keep up the pretense. "Sure. Let's go."

He slipped his arm over her shoulders and together they left. Lisa knew the act was for his family's sake, but for a small, exultant moment she pretended he had done it because he wanted to.

Chapter Seven

"Lisa, breakfast is on."

Dylan's voice on the other side of her bedroom door gave Lisa a start. She'd been standing in front of the mirror in her bathroom for the past ten minutes, trying to tame her unruly curls.

"Be right there," she called out, pulling a face at the tangle she'd managed to create.

Not that it mattered what she looked like, she thought, wrinkling her nose at her reflection. She wasn't trying to impress anyone.

Or was she?

Two days ago, before the wedding and before the church service, Dylan had simply been an overly attractive single boss.

Now, forty-eight hours later, Lisa felt as if all the barriers she thought she had put in place against his charm had been breached by his attentiveness. By seeing him with his family. By pretending to be a part of it by being his girlfriend.

She thought of the church service yesterday. For so many years she'd blamed God for her parents' death. But yesterday she had felt as if God was waiting. As if the breach between them was of no matter to Him. All she had to do was trust Him.

Could she?

"You coming?" Another knock on the door pulled her back from her reverie.

"I'm coming." Lisa turned away from the girl in the mirror and her very serious thoughts and joined Dylan in the hallway.

"Did you sleep well?" he asked, his smile warm, welcoming.

She nodded, suddenly shy around him.

The shrill ring of a cell phone from her room shot straight to her heart. It could only be Gabe. She had promised him she would call him last night and give him a update. She had forgotten.

"You going to get that?" Dylan asked.

"I'll meet you downstairs." She gave him a quick smile and walked into her bedroom, shutting the door firmly behind her.

"What have you found out?" Gabe's voice rang through the cell phone. Lisa glanced over her shoulder, hoping Dylan was gone.

"Nothing yet." She kept her voice low as she walked into the half bath, feeling like a criminal.

"What has Dara given you?"

"Just the invoices and purchase orders for the past six months."

"You won't find anything there. She's decoying you. You need to get into the office."

"How do you know?" And once again Lisa's suspicions flared.

"You sound like you doubt me." Gabe's voice rose a notch.

"I don't, Gabe. You know that."

"I don't know that anymore. You haven't been to see me in two days."

"Gabe, I've been kind of tied up."

He was silent a moment. "With Dylan? At Stanley Park?"

His words sent her heart into her stomach. "How did you know?"

"I phoned the house to ask for you. Someone told me you were at the Park. So I took the bus down there. I saw you with him."

Lisa closed her eyes, pressing the cell phone against her ear. "Gabe you can't phone here for me. If these people find out that you're my brother..."

"You and Dylan won't be so cozy anymore, will you?"

"Stop it, Gabe," she snapped, suddenly impatient with her brother. "I'm doing what I can and I'm doing it all for you." She took a slow breath, trying to calm her beating heart. Time to move on to another topic. "How is work going?"

Silence.

"Gabe, what's wrong?"

"I'm thinking of quitting."

Lisa's heart started right up again, memories of

other disappointments crowding in on her devotion to her brother. "Don't do that, Gabe. Please."

"Lisa, it's a dead-end job. The pay sucks and the work is boring. I've met up with some guy who runs a shipping company. He needs a part-time accountant."

In his overly optimistic voice Lisa heard echoes of other opportunities that had sounded too good to be true. "I thought you said you couldn't get another accounting job without a reference."

"Well, this guy doesn't need a reference."

"Shouldn't that tell you something?" Lisa closed her eyes. And prayed. "Gabe, I'll come see you as soon as possible. Maybe tonight. Please. Don't quit yet. Something will happen here. I know it."

His silence pressed heavily down on her.

But Lisa knew how Gabe's thoughts went and how impatient he could be. "Hang in there," she said, struggling to sound positive. "I'll come see you tonight."

He sighed. "Okay," he said, reluctance edging his voice.

Lisa closed her cell phone and sighed lightly. *Dear Lord,* she prayed, *I don't deserve to talk to You, but please take care of Gabe. Please don't let him do anything silly.*

It was such a short prayer. And uttered so spontaneously. Yet Lisa felt a gentle peace surround her.

Dylan was already hunched over his desk, fruit and a bagel on a plate at his elbow. He looked up when she came in. "I thought I would get started." He held her gaze a moment, a soft smile curving his lips. Thankfully he didn't ask her about the phone call.

Lisa put a plate of food together and joined Dylan in the study. She sat down at the computer and worked at finishing the job she'd started on Friday.

Though her attention was on her work, she couldn't help the occasional glance Dylan's way. One time he was looking at her, but as soon as their eyes met, he looked away.

Lisa didn't want to read anything into it. Couldn't.

She was finished and walked over to Dylan's table and pulled another file. A piece of paper, stuck to one of the files, fell to the floor.

Dylan picked it up, wrinkling his nose. "This thing's a mess." It was crumpled and stained with rings from a coffee cup. "Does it look like anything?"

Lisa took the folded-over piece of paper from him. "Looks to me like messy bookkeeping. It was just stuck to one of the files," she replied. She tried to peel the folds apart. "I could try steaming them."

"I can do it."

"I don't mind. I need the break."

"The kettle is in the pots-and-pans cupboard beside the stove," Dylan said.

The kitchen was empty, and Lisa easily found the kettle, surprised that Dylan would know. When she and Gabe had lived together, the only pan he'd been able to find was the frying pan, and that was because it was always in the sink or on the stove.

While the water was boiling she tried one more

time to pry apart the folds of paper with a knife, but succeeded only in ripping it a bit more.

The steam was pouring out of the kettle now and she held the paper above it, careful to avoid burning her hand. The paper slowly crinkled away until she could unfold it.

It was an invoice. Inside was another paper, a memo to Dara. In Gabe's handwriting.

"Don't know if I can keep doing this," Lisa read. "Ted needs to know."

Her heart skittered, and deep inside she felt as if something had been yanked out, torn up by the roots. The words shouted at her.

Keep doing this? Doing what? And what did Ted need to know?

Lisa lowered the memo, her hands shaking. Her first reaction was to crumple up the paper and throw it in the garbage. Her second was to grab it and run across town to her brother to ask what it meant.

She glanced quickly around the kitchen, then folded the paper and slipped it into the back pocket of her pants. She couldn't let anyone see this until she had talked to Gabe about it.

She doubted Dylan could have seen the memo. It was smaller than the invoice and tucked right inside, no edges showing.

She smoothed out the invoice, her fingers trembling. Pulling in a long, steadying breath, she walked back to the study, hoping, praying her face didn't reveal any of her doubts and fears.

Dylan glanced up when she came back. "Anything important?"

"Just another invoice." The lie didn't come easily to her, but Dylan didn't seem to notice her discomfort.

"I was hoping it would be something more exciting than that," Dylan said with a light laugh.

"Me, too." Lisa spun away, pretending to be engrossed in the paper, the crinkle in her back pocket sounding as loud as gunshots in the quiet of the study.

She sat down and laid the innocent invoice on her desk. She glanced at the name of the customer and on a sticky note jotted down the customer name.

"I just need to run upstairs a moment," she said, glancing at Dylan, wishing her cheeks weren't so flushed.

Dylan looked up. Smiled at her. "Sure."

Lisa walked out of the room, then ran up the stairs. As she slipped into her bedroom she felt more and more like a criminal. Was she stealing? Was she as bad as her brother?

As she hid the memo in her suitcase, she stifled a surge of guilt. She would show Dylan once she had talked to Gabe. Once she found out what had really happened.

Three hours later Dylan pushed himself away from the table he was working at and came to stand beside Lisa.

"Well, I'm done here. How are you making out?"

Lisa jumped, then glanced up at him. Look casual.

"I've married all the invoices to the purchase orders," she said. "And from what I've seen everything fits."

"So nothing there."

"Not in this file." She took a breath and took a chance. "I think we need to get into the office files and computers. It would be faster for one thing, and easier for Dara," she said, hoping her voice sounded more casual than she felt. What if he asked her why? What would she say?

Dylan tapped his pen on the desk. "I think you're right." He slipped his hand through his hair and leaned back against the desk. He glanced down at Lisa, his teeth catching one side of his lip. "Do you get the feeling this is a waste of time?"

"Ted seemed to agree with you."

"I get the feeling Ted wants nothing more than for me to get myself out of here and back to Toronto." Dylan sighed and pushed himself away from the desk. "Which makes me want to go see what we can find at the office."

Thirty-five minutes later they were escorted into an office adjoining a large warehouse. The reception area was spacious and light, furnished in much the same fashion as the Matheson home. Large impressionist paintings hung on the wall. The sparse furniture had a European look.

"Can you tell that Mom redid this place, as well?" Dylan murmured to Lisa as he opened the large smoked-glass door for her. "Same down-home country atmosphere."

Lisa stifled a quick laugh. "Your mother has exquisite taste," she said quietly. "Maybe you should get her to come and do something with your office in Toronto.''

''Even if I was staying with Matheson Telecom, I wouldn't. It's not my style.''

They approached the receptionist half-hidden behind a waist-high sweep of metal and glass. She glanced up, her eyes flicking over Lisa, then coming to rest on Dylan. Her smile changed as she reached up and smoothed her hair. ''Hello, Mr. Matheson. Your father is in,'' she said, leaning slightly forward. Her shining eyes and breathy voice exuded a welcome Lisa was sure she didn't extend to just anyone who walked in the door. The secretary smiled again, and Lisa felt a surprising pinch of jealousy.

''Lisa and I will just go straight in.'' Dylan glanced her way and smiled at her. A spark of previous emotions flashed through her. When Dylan had danced with her.

Lisa wrenched her gaze away, reaching for control.

She was almost there when they walked past Alex's secretary into Alex's office and saw Alex at his desk.

And Dylan dropped his arm over her shoulder.

It's just an act, she reminded herself even as she felt the gentle flush of connection at the warmth of his arm.

''Dylan. Lisa. So nice to see you here.'' Alex got up, the delight in his voice showing Lisa even more than his beaming smile how pleased he was to see them together. ''Are you two touring around?''

Dylan's fingers tightened on her shoulder, but he

didn't take up his father's invitation. "We don't have time, Dad. We're here to check out some files in the office."

Alex tapped his fingers lightly on the desk. "I'll have to talk to Dara about it."

When Alex left, Lisa edged away from Dylan. Thankfully he got the hint and lowered his arm. Which, to Lisa's dismay, didn't make her feel any more comfortable than before.

She walked over to a set of chairs flanked by tables. Brochures lay on the table advertising the various products handled by Matheson Telecom and Lisa picked one up, pretending interest in it.

Gabe's phone call this morning had left her jittery and out of sorts. The memo only added to it.

But as she glanced at Dylan, who still stood in the center of the room watching her, she knew there was another cause.

The tentative advance and retreat happening between her and Dylan was more than the show they were putting on for the sake of his family. Last night no one had been around and she had felt the pull of attraction, gently irresistible and seemingly innocent.

At the same time she didn't dare give in. Her secret hung between them like a menacing shadow. Sooner or later it would come out, and anything they had shared to that point would be swept away.

Later, later.

"I can't seem to find Dara." Alex came back, looking apologetic. "I was so sure she was here today."

"All we need to do is look at the most recent files,

Dad,'' Dylan said, his voice edged with anger. ''Surely Dara doesn't need to be around for that.''

Alex glanced at Lisa, then at Dylan, raising his hands palm up in a gesture of surrender. ''I'm sorry, Dylan. If you had called before you came, you might have caught her. She knows where they are.''

''What about Ted? Surely he can help us.''

''Ted was never that involved in the bookkeeping.''

''Which was part of the problem,'' Dylan said.

''Dylan, please…'' Alex held his hand up in a placating gesture. ''This will all get solved sooner or later. We just need time.''

Dylan clenched one hand into a fist and tapped it against his side. Lisa echoed his frustration both with Dara and Alex. Why was he being so evasive? Was he protecting Dara, as well?

And in that moment Lisa understood Dylan's discontent with his father's relationship to him.

Yet threaded through that was her conversation with Alex only yesterday morning. His wish that one of his sons would make wise and good choices.

Something else was going on. She couldn't figure out what, but somehow it hinged on Alex. And what kind of choices he was going to make.

''So we're just supposed to sit around and twiddle our thumbs while we wait for Dara to decide whether or not she's going to give us access to her office?'' Dylan's question was surprisingly quiet, but Lisa felt his exasperation.

Alex smiled a sad smile. ''No. You're supposed to be on holiday.''

Dylan blew out his breath in an exasperated sigh. "Dad, you asked me to come and help you figure this problem out. I'm trying to do that, but not getting a lot of cooperation from either you or Dara. And Ted doesn't have a clue what's going on. I hope this isn't an elaborate waste of Lisa's and my time."

"You have to believe me when I say it is making a difference, Dylan. But today you won't be able to do anything. Why don't you take a break for now." He smiled at Lisa. "Take Lisa out on the boat. The work will keep for an afternoon. Trust me, it will all come together. Hopefully soon."

Dylan shook his head, his shoulders sagging lightly as if in defeat. "I guess that's the crux of the matter, isn't it, Dad? Trust. You should give some serious thought to how you want us to proceed."

Alex almost winced. "Can we carry on this conversation some other time?" he asked quietly.

"I've nothing more to say. For now." Dylan glanced at Lisa and held his hand out to her. "I guess we have the afternoon free."

What could she do but take it?

As his fingers wrapped around hers, his eyes held her gaze. "So, what do you think of going sailing?"

Lisa swallowed down the sudden uplifting rush of pleasure. She was supposed to be helping Gabe. But as Alex had said, they couldn't right now.

But could she afford to spend the afternoon with Dylan? And what would Gabe say when he found out?

"Go ahead, Lisa," Alex urged. "Dylan's an excellent sailor. You can trust him."

Dylan threw his father a puzzled glance, then with a shrug turned back to Lisa. "What do you say?" he asked, his voice pitched low.

Lisa felt the intimacy of his tone, was drawn into the intensity of his gaze and against her better judgment said yes.

"So which one is your dad's boat?" Lisa asked, staring through the forest of masts bobbing up and down in the marina. The sun flashed off pristine hulls, gleaming chrome and brass overwhelming the tiny flashes shot off by the water.

"It's the sloop on slip E over there. I doubt you'd be able to see it, though."

Lisa stood on tiptoe, scanning the various boats, then nodded. "Oh, yes. There it is."

Dylan jerked his head around, frowning his puzzlement. "How do you…" Then he caught the joke. "Very smart. And what do you think of the ketch beside it?"

Unable to stop the mischief that had caught hold of her, Lisa rolled her eyes in mock disgust. It was as if getting away from his family and from his work had allowed them to choose their relationship. And she was tired of intensity and seriousness.

"Like I don't know my boats. Look at its mast. That's no ketch."

"And it is a…" Dylan prompted, picking up on her mood.

"If you don't know, I'm not going to enlighten you," she said with an airy wave of her hand.

Dylan tugged on the brim of her hat, pulling it

lower over her eyes. "We'll see how cocky you are once you're out on the water," he said with a grin.

As she followed him along the dock she felt the tensions of the morning drift away with the light breeze that teased her hair.

She breathed in the peculiar scent of the harbor—water, the faint scent of diesel and the underlying smell of fish. Gulls wheeled above, taunting them with their strident cries. Below them, water gurgled against the pilings, slapped the hulls of the boats.

It was going to be a glorious day.

"This one, right?" Dylan said, stopping in front of a midsize boat. It looked to be about thirty feet long, its mast stretching far above them.

She glanced at the prow of the boat and saw *The Stephanie* written in flowing cursive. "You're more percipient than you look," she said with a grin.

"And percipient enough not to use that word instead of perceptive, which is what it really means."

"I rest my case," Lisa said with a grin. "So this is the vessel."

"It's not a big boat, but it handles like a dream," Dylan said. He untied a line and climbed up into the boat. "Hand me the gear and then I'll help you on."

Lisa gave him the thermos and cooler holding food that the housekeeper deemed necessary for a trip out on the boat. Then Dylan held out his hand.

Lisa's hesitation was minute.

"You don't have to be afraid," he said, smiling his encouragement. "The boat won't tip. I promise."

She took his hand, but was disappointed by how quickly he let go of her hand. As he unlocked what looked like a small door broken into three parts, Lisa glanced upward. The tiny flag at the top of the mast seemed impossibly high.

Her stomach lurched and she grabbed the nearest rope to steady herself.

''What's wrong?'' Dylan asked.

''How are you going to get that sail all the way up that mast by yourself?''

''I'll use the halyard on the main and the furlings on the jib.''

''Furling. Is that like a small furlong?'' she joked, trying to cover up her nervousness and her lack of knowledge. She had never been on a boat before. And now she was going to allow Dylan to take her out onto the ocean?

Dylan laughed, sliding the boards up and setting them aside. ''Come down below a moment. We can put the food away and I can give you the grand tour.''

Lisa rubbed her damp palms against her pant legs and followed Dylan through the narrow entrance and down the ladder to a small room belowdecks. A family picture hung on a short wall above a small couch built into the side of the boat. The kitchen had a small stove with an oven, a sink and counter and cupboards directly above them. Everything a person needed for a long trip.

''Okay, landlubber,'' Dylan said, glancing around. ''A few lessons. The front of the boat is the bow, the back is the stern. If you're hungry, you can make something in the galley. Behind you is the head, self-explanatory if you take a look, and to get back up to the cockpit you clamber up the companionway.''

Lisa blinked, trying to absorb the information Dylan seemed to take delight in deluging her with.

''Since this is belowdecks, I'm assuming a whole other vocabulary awaits me once we go up the—'' she gestured to the ladder behind Dylan ''—companionway.''

''We haven't even started on mainsails, jibs, lines and sheets.''

Lisa grinned. ''Just tell me when I'm supposed to say, 'Avast, me hearties' and I'll try to keep up,'' she said, looking around the snug interior of the boat. ''This is cozy,'' she added.

Dylan tapped a pole leading up from the floor of the interior, looking around, as well. ''I've spent a lot of happy hours on this boat.''

Lisa didn't think she imagined the wistful tone in his voice. ''Did you go with your family?''

''Mostly just me and my dad,'' he said quietly, looking past her as if seeing other memories.

Lisa stopped the questions that almost spilled out. It wasn't any of her business. She didn't need to tangle herself any deeper in the affairs of this family.

Yet a gentle sorrow seeped through her for the hurt she heard in his voice. An echo of the regret in his father's voice when he spoke of Dylan.

''I have to check the engine room,'' Dylan said. ''You can go above deck and enjoy the weather.''

As he moved to pass her, their eyes met. He slowed, she didn't move and awareness sparked be-

tween them. In the close quarters it was almost palpable.

Stop this now.

Lisa pulled her gaze away, turned and escaped up
the companionway into the sunshine above. As she
sat down on the bench beside the wheel, she took a
long slow breath.

Dylan's movements below set the boat rocking
lightly.

She shouldn't have come here. Shouldn't be
spending this personal time with Dylan. She was
trespassing over the boundaries she had set herself,
moving into a place that would be too hard to escape.

A gull's cry pulled her attention away from her
disquiet, and the slight rocking motion of the boat
soothed her anxiety.

It was just a short sailing trip. When would she
ever have a chance to experience that?

The day was going to be just fine, she assured
herself, the tension easing from her shoulders. What
was happening between her and Dylan was simply a
product of spending more time together than she had
with any man for a long time.

As long as she was aware of that, she could handle
it.

Chapter Eight

Dylan turned on the fuel, opened the sea cock and ran through the usual presailing check. His movements were sure, practiced, old habits slipping back as easily as putting on worn shoes.

The routine alleviated the moment of tension created by the allure of Lisa.

The vessel that had once seemed roomy enough with four people aboard now seemed cramped and crowded. He and Lisa would constantly be bumping into each other, and from her reaction a moment ago he sensed she would be the one constantly pulling away.

He wrote the barometer reading and closed the log book with a light laugh at his own whimsy. Her reaction shouldn't concern him. It was just a day away from work, that was all.

It was the thought of taking the boat out, not being

with Lisa, that quickened his heart, he reassured himself.

It had been a long time since he had gone sailing. In Toronto all his time was spent at Matheson Telecom, to the detriment of many relationships and his leisure time.

And now he was moving to another company where he would have to prove his worth.

Dylan pushed the thought aside as he switched on the radio and listened. Shipping traffic sounded light. He quickly checked the weather. All the pieces were in place for a perfect day. Enjoy the moment, he thought as he clambered up the companionway.

He started the engine. The motor turned over immediately with a muted growl.

"Lisa, do me a favor," he said, checking the gauges. "Look over the stern and see if water is coming out of the exhaust."

The boat rocked slightly as Lisa moved and leaned over. "I see water pouring out from something."

"Good. Thanks."

"Water coming out of a boat is a good thing?"

Dylan glanced up at the worry in her voice. Smiled at her comical expression. "Water comes in from the sea and goes into the cooling part of the engine, then out the exhaust. Like air flowing past the radiator of a car."

"Landlubber question coming up," she said, sitting down again. "If this is a sailboat, why do you have an engine in it?"

"It's much easier to maneuver out of the marina

with a motor than a sail. And quicker.'' He pulled out a life jacket. ''Here. Put this on.''

Lisa held up the lime-green personal flotation device and pulled her lower lip between her teeth. ''You realize, of course, this color is going to totally wash out my complexion.''

Dylan laughed, thankful once again for Lisa's easy humor, always ready at hand. ''Better your complexion than having you washed overboard.''

''Just how far are you planning to go? Tokyo?''

''I guess we'll see where the day takes us.'' He jumped off the boat and untied the spring lines, then the bow and stern line and got back on. He put away the lines and took his place behind the wheel of the boat.

As they motored out of the marina, Dylan could feel the tensions of the past week ease away, soothed by the movement of the boat, the light breeze on his face. The promise of a beautiful day of sailing ahead canceled out the puzzle of his father's actions.

''This is the most I've seen you smile since I've met you,'' Lisa said, angling him a grin.

''I've missed this,'' he said quietly, navigating his way through the throngs of boats.

''Toronto is on the water. Didn't you ever go sailing there?''

''No time.''

''Are you going to have time at your next job?''

Her casual comment hit a vulnerable spot. ''I'll be busy.'' He would be going nuts, he amended. Starting over. Trying to prove himself.

Was he doing the right thing?

It was too late for second thoughts, but they hovered in his mind nonetheless.

"Mr. Upwardly Mobile," Lisa teased. "Ted doesn't seem to work as hard as you do."

"Ted is his own person," Dylan said, hoping his reply sounded more forgiving than he usually felt toward his older brother.

Lisa pushed her billed cap farther back on her head, as if to see Dylan better. "I get the feeling you're not filled with fraternal devotion to Ted."

"Fraternal," he said, flashing her a teasing glance. "Most people would say brotherly."

"It is related to brothers. From the Latin word *frater* meaning brother. Also connected to fraternity."

"You like fooling with words, don't you?"

Lisa smiled, lifting her face to the light wind. "Among other things."

She didn't elaborate and Dylan was content to leave her to her little secrets. He knew there were more. One being the person who had called her a couple of times on her cell phone, whom she never talked about. He was also fairly certain she had gone visiting the same person the evening of the rehearsal party he had attended alone.

She had told him at the interview that she was unattached. So who was this mystery person?

"So when do you hoist the mizzenmast?"

Dylan pulled his attention back to Lisa. "This is a sloop. Only has one mast. A boat with three masts has a mizzenmast, and you only hoist sails."

"Oh, that's right. I read that somewhere," she

said, snapping her fingers. "Did you ever sail a boat with more than one mast?"

Dylan shook his head. "We had a larger boat than this at one time, but it still only had one mast. Dad traded it off on this smaller boat because the rest of the family seldom came along." He couldn't help but smile, remembering how relieved his sisters had been that they no longer had to be coerced into coming along. He could never understand their reluctance. To him, sailing had been the ultimate release. A place to get away from the stress and tension of school.

The one place he and his father were on equal footing.

"So you and your dad sailed a lot?"

"Almost every chance we could get." Dylan turned the boat into the wind and slowed the engine. "Come here. I need your help now."

Lisa pointed to herself. "Me. As in this landlubber?"

"This is easy. Just hold the wheel exactly where it is. I need to pull up the mainsail and unfurl the jib."

Lisa got up, suddenly looking nervous. He moved over so she could take the wheel.

"Don't look so tense," he joked.

"I'm not tense," she replied. "Just terribly and extremely alert."

"You don't have to white-knuckle it." Dylan let go as soon as she had the wheel. "Just hold it right where you have it. Nice and steady." He waited a moment. "You okay?"

"I'm fine. You just go unfurl some sails."

Her bottom lip was clamped between her teeth and a deep frown pulled her eyebrows together. He was about to make another comment, but kept it to himself. Once she saw that the boat wasn't going to take off, she'd be fine.

In a matter of moments he had the mainsail up. He untied the furling line and pulled the jib sheet.

The sails started undulating as they caught their first taste of the wind.

"Dylan. What's going on?" Lisa's voice had flown up an octave. "Those sails aren't supposed to flap like that, are they?"

"They're just filling up," he called back, unable to stop laughing. "Just steer to port."

"Office language, please."

"Your left."

As he worked his way back, the sails, seemingly satisfied with what was offered, filled with a snap. The tug pushed Dylan's heart against his chest, the familiar expectation of exhilaration sending his blood singing through his veins.

"This boat is tilting. Is it supposed to tilt like this?"

Dylan came up beside her and let her struggle along a moment. "You're doing great, Lisa. A natural."

"Well, it's been fun, but I have to scream now. Please take over."

"Here. Let me help you."

He stood behind her, placed his hands over hers and gently corrected their course.

She drew in a deep breath, but to his surprise didn't pull away. Of course, as tightly as her hands were wrapped around the wheel, he doubted she was able to move at all.

"It's not as hard as it looks," he said as her hair tickled his chin. She smelled as fresh as sea air, with a hint of feminine sweetness. "Just keep the boat pointed in this direction for now and we'll be fine."

The boat skimmed over the water, the pull of the sail singing through the lines. Dylan's spirits responded, thrilling to the faint groan of the boat, the tautness of the sail.

Lisa hadn't moved since he had come up behind her, but her hands no longer held the wheel in a death grip. He couldn't see her face, but could feel her slowly relaxing.

"It goes pretty fast," she murmured, still holding on to the wheel.

"The wind isn't even that strong today. Sometimes this boat just flies." Dylan shifted his weight, his arms brushing hers. "You didn't put on your life jacket."

"I'm a good swimmer."

Dylan didn't push the point. Once they got farther out, he would have to insist she put it on. But for now he didn't want her to move. Wanted to enjoy the feeling of protecting her. Sheltering her.

And so far she didn't seem to mind him standing right behind her.

They sped away from the harbor and swooped under Lions Gate Bridge.

"This is a very different vantage point than when

I first came here,'' she said, her head tilting up to look at the bridge as they sailed under it. "You promised you'd take me sailing when we drove over that bridge. And here I am.''

Dylan looked down at her upturned face. A dimple danced beside her mouth and her eyes shimmered, turning a soft hazel in the sunlight. When her head bumped his shoulder, her eyes swung around to his and a mixture of emotions tumbled across her face. He caught a glimpse of yearning that called to his own loneliness.

Without stopping to think or analyze the right or wrong, he caught her chin with one hand, turning her face a fraction toward his.

She shifted her body ever so slightly toward him. Rested her head back against his shoulder.

When Dylan lowered his mouth to hers, she didn't move or resist.

The boat straightened. Lisa pulled away. "What's happening?''

"Got distracted,'' Dylan murmured, catching the wheel and turning it back to starboard. As the sails filled again, Dylan glanced down at Lisa.

She hadn't moved away from him. Dylan took a chance and placed his hands over hers and rested his chin lightly on her head.

Just as when they'd danced at Chelsea's wedding he couldn't banish the sense of rightness he felt. As if every silly thing in the world would make more sense if only they could stay this way. Together.

He brushed his chin over her head, unable to suppress his good humor. He had never had feelings like this for any woman he had ever been with.

Yet he knew less about her than he did about any of the other women he had dated.

The unwelcome thought lurked on the edges of his mind and he suppressed it. Pushed aside his second thoughts.

He had a beautiful woman in his arms. He had favorable winds, a warm sun and open water ahead of him.

It was as close to perfection as he could expect.

Lisa didn't want to move. In fact, if she could have her way, time would stop, would remain in this moment while she savored every nuance, every image.

The fresh smell of the water breaking away from the boat, the faint groaning of the lines holding the sail, the warmth of the sun.

Dylan's arms around her creating a haven of safety. They didn't have an audience now, so there was no need to pretend.

And what about your own pretense?

Lisa bit her lip as guilt crowded out the peace of the moment. Things were starting to overlap, feelings seeping out around loyalty.

She was standing in the arms of the kind of man she had dreamed of since she was a young girl. A man who had the kind of family she had always wanted.

And if they found out who she was, it would all disappear as quickly as fog when the sun came out.

Dear Lord, what have I started? How can I fix all this?

Her prayer was born of a desperation to find a way to satisfy her own conscience, newly aroused by the church service the other day. She needed to help her brother. She wanted to be a part of Dylan's life.

But she couldn't do both.

"Thanks for the lesson," she murmured, ducking under Dylan's arm. She felt suddenly chilled and slipped her sweater on. And then her life jacket.

She didn't look at Dylan. Instead she concentrated on the water, squinting against the light dancing on the waves.

Another sailboat surged past them, the laughter of the occupants following in its wake. Lisa pretended to be intent on its progress, envying the people their light spirits.

How had her life gotten so complicated? Her plan had seemed so easy before she went for the interview. Find information. Help her brother. Foolish of her to think that she could take this all on herself.

She blinked against a surprising onslaught of tears.

I've been foolish, Lord. I've been stubborn and I've been proud, she prayed. *Please forgive me. Help me get through this. Show me what I should do.* Her prayer was a muddle of questions, a confusion of thoughts. Yet, as before, she felt a gentle peace cover her. Nothing had been solved, but she no longer felt alone.

"Are you okay?" Dylan's voice broke into her thoughts and she turned to face him, her smile genuine now.

"I think so."

He frowned at her cryptic response, but thankfully didn't press her.

Lisa drew on old coping skills honed with each move she and Gabe had made to a new foster home. New situations and emotions.

This was where she was at the moment. She didn't need to think back or ahead. She had to control the things she was directly involved in right now.

She turned her face up to the sky, soaking in the warmth of the sun and allowing herself pleasure in the feel of the movement of the boat dancing over the water. The jagged mountains edging the harbor set a romantic counterpoint, clearly underlining the uniqueness of this time and place.

She chanced another look at Dylan. He stood on the deck, feet slightly apart, his hands resting lightly on the wheel. He looked more relaxed than he had since she had met him.

"So if we're heading away from Vancouver with the wind at our back, how do we get back?" she asked, trying to lighten the tone of the afternoon.

Dylan angled her a smile. "Maybe we won't. What would you think of that?"

The teasing comment tantalized her, bringing back all the emotions of the kiss they had shared. A kiss she shouldn't have allowed to happen.

She thought of the two of them staying here, in this self-contained place—each surge of the boat pulling them farther away from Vancouver and the complications of their lives there.

It was too compelling a thought and she couldn't reply.

"What would you miss?" Dylan asked, carrying on the fantasy.

Lisa leaned over the side, watching the flow of water streaming past the boat.

She'd miss her brother, but she couldn't tell Dylan that. What else did she have to miss? "I'd probably miss my blow-dryer," she said with a grin. "Maybe my thesaurus. How about you?"

Dylan shrugged, looping his forearms over the wheel, looking straight ahead. "I don't use a blow-dryer."

"Just pomade, I understand. I bet you'd miss your family, though."

"Probably."

"Your mother, your father?" Lisa couldn't stop herself. Each time she saw Alex and Dylan the strain between them bothered her more and more.

"I suppose I'd miss him, too."

"You *suppose* you'd miss your father? That seems a strange way to say it."

Dylan rested his chin on his stacked hands, the faint breeze teasing his hair. He sighed deeply. "I love my dad. I just don't love what he does."

"And what does he do?"

Dylan didn't answer for a moment and Lisa kept silent, content to let the moment draw itself out.

"You know the story of the prodigal son?" he asked. "From the Bible?"

"My stepfather read it to me a couple of times,"

Lisa said. "Next to the story of Joseph it was one of my favorites."

"Did you ever feel sorry for the older brother?" Dylan tilted his head, held her gaze.

Lisa paused, pondering that thought. "Sometimes. A little bit."

"I always did. I could never figure out why Jesus had to make that poor guy out to be the bad example."

"Well, he was the ungrateful one." Lisa leaned forward, then sat up as her life jacket dug in to her knees and the back of her neck. "He wasn't happy to see his brother come back."

Dylan noticed her discomfort. "You can take your life jacket off it you want."

Lisa had donned the flotation device as a feeble protection after Dylan had kissed her. "That's okay. I feel safer with it on." She realized the double entrendre too late. "So why do you sympathize with the older brother?"

"Because in many ways, I'm him," Dylan continued, looking back at the boat. "Birth order aside, of course."

"Ted being the wastrel, I take it."

Dylan laughed. Corrected his course. "I have lost track of how many times my father has given Ted second chances."

"Your father is a good man. I think he's fair and trustworthy. It's that quality that makes him do that."

"My father broke trust with me when he put Ted in charge of the company here in Vancouver."

The suppressed anger in his voice made her wince. "Ted is the older brother."

"That was my father's reason, as well." Dylan straightened. "Anyway, that doesn't concern me as much as it used to. Once I'm back on my own, the company can slide down the tubes the way it's going now."

"Surely the company isn't doing that badly."

Dylan shrugged. "Maybe not, but Ted has never been leadership material. The fact that money had gone missing for so long doesn't say much about his control of either his wife or the company."

Lisa felt a flare of hope. "What do you mean, control of his wife?"

"She's the one who hired that accountant. He worked under her so in a way I hold her responsible for his actions."

Don't know if I can keep doing this. Ted needs to know.

Lisa felt as if the words on Gabe's memo were burned on her forehead for Dylan and all the world to see. "So you don't know if Ted was in charge or if Dara was in charge."

"I don't know if Ted has ever been in charge of anything."

Lisa knew she did not imagine the tone of bitterness in Dylan's voice. "Surely Ted must have been able to do *something*. Why else would your father give him so much responsibility?"

"My father has always had a soft spot for Ted, and Ted has used that to his advantage. All my life I've tried to live up to Dad's expectations. But it hasn't done me any good.'' Dylan flashed Lisa a casual smile. "And now that's enough about my brother, my father and all the other things in my life that I can't control.''

Dylan's comment reflected feelings so close to hers that Lisa felt a flash of connection. "That makes me think about what the minister was talking about on Sunday. About letting go.''

"That's one thing about religion I've always had the hardest time with. Letting go. Letting God." Dylan spun the wheel of the boat. "I guess that's why I stopped going to church.''

"I used to go to church," Lisa said softly, looking at the islands ahead of them. "Me and my family.''

"Did you enjoy it?''

Lisa nodded. "My mother and I seldom went when I was growing up. When Rick and—'' she stumbled, almost mentioning Gabe's name "—and my mother got married, he was a strong Christian, so we all started going.'' She bit back the flow of words—her nervousness making her chatty.

"So what made you want to go with my family?''

Lisa pulled her legs up, pressing her knees against the bulk of the life jacket. She cast about for the right way to articulate her reasons. "A promise I'd made.'' And that was all she was going to tell him.

"Yet you seemed sad in church.''

Lisa only nodded. That day in church Dylan had given her his hankie to wipe her tears. He was probably wondering what that had been about. But she couldn't tell him. Couldn't share the sorrow she felt over her fractured life. Her parents dead. Gabe living in a dumpy apartment and all the while she was lying to one of the kindest families she had ever met.

"I missed my parents," she said simply, surprising herself at her confession. "I didn't think I had any more tears in me, honestly. It's been ten years since they died."

"It's okay to be sad. It shows you loved them."

"I enjoyed the service, too, though." Through it all she had heard God calling her. Drawing her back into a relationship with Him. The only one that mattered.

"What did you like about it?"

"It would be easier if I said it was nostalgia," she said. "The sort of thing happy families do. You know, the Norman Rockwell calendar pictures. But it was more than that. I realized I missed God."

He didn't respond to that. Their silence was broken only by the swish of water against the hull of the boat, the faint groaning of the mast and the line, holding the wind in the sails. A gull wheeled overhead, its piercing cry adding a melancholy note to the day.

After a while Lisa let her gaze wander around, over to Dylan. To her astonishment and discomfort, he was looking directly at her.

"You continually surprise me, Lisa Sterling," he said quietly. "Just when I think I know who you are, something else comes up."

"Better to be a surprise than a shock, I guess," Lisa said, her forced laugh pushing away the gentle intimacy of his remark.

"You might be that, too."

Foreboding slivered through her at his oblique comment. If he only knew....

She hugged her knees tighter, the plastic buckle of the life jacket digging in to her legs. A small penance for her evasions and secrets.

Enough, enough. She was doing what she had to do. Her first priority was Gabe.

"Tomorrow is my parents' anniversary party," Dylan said after a while. "You still up to going?"

She realized he was giving her a gracious out, and for a flicker of a heartbeat she was tempted to take it. "I promised to come to both events—the wedding and the anniversary," she said, resting her chin on her knees. "I like to keep my promises."

In her peripheral vision she saw Dylan nodding his head, the faint breeze teasing his hair around his face. "I sensed that about you. You are an honorable person, Lisa."

She didn't allow herself to follow that comment through. She shifted in her seat.

"You getting bored?" he asked.

She quirked a challenging grin at him. "What if I say yes?"

"Then I'll make you unbored." Dylan winked at her, spun the wheel and pulled in two lines. The boat listed and sped up. "Hang on and lean back. We're going for broke."

Lisa clamped one hand over her mouth, stifling a squeal as the boat lurched. Dylan laughed aloud, a spray of water flecking his hair.

But Lisa said nothing, her heart thrumming with a mixture of anxiety and exhilaration as she clung to the boat. They went faster, skimming over the water, the hull thumping over the waves, the sound getting louder.

Dylan flashed a grin at her, as if taunting her. On they raced, the boat tilting so far that all Lisa saw when she looked down from her perch was the deep gray water rushing past the boat.

Dylan looked like a pirate, his shirt billowing around him, his hair falling over his face as he held the wheel. Water sprayed as they flew over the water, and Lisa laughed out loud in sheer pleasure.

She didn't want him to stop. She wanted this mad rush of freedom to take them away from Vancouver and the complications of their lives back there. Just her and Dylan.

When Dylan finally eased the sheets and the boat slowed, Lisa felt a thrum of disappointment.

"I'm impressed, Lisa," Dylan said. "I thought for sure you were going to yell at me to stop."

"No. It was great." Lisa couldn't stop grinning. "What a rush."

Their eyes met. Held by the shared experience. And when Dylan held out one hand to her, Lisa didn't even stop to think. She slipped off her seat, took his hand and let him pull her to his side.

Then she let him kiss her again.

And this time she gave in to an impulse and lifted her hand to his head. Slipped her fingers through his thick, dark hair and let herself pretend that all this— the kiss, Dylan, this moment—was normal.

She didn't want to contemplate how this would

end. For now she had this moment and she intended to treasure it. To savor it.

A memory for her to draw on when this was all over.

Chapter Nine

"Okay, Lisa, who is this man and what did you do with my brother?" Ted stood in the side doorway of his parents' house, barring Dylan's and Lisa's entrance. He grinned at his own joke, his hazel eyes flicking over them both in unwelcome speculation. "The Dylan Matheson I know would never play hooky and go sailing in the middle of a weekday no matter how pretty the girl. And he's been with enough."

The afternoon had been so wonderful, so entirely perfect, Ted's insinuations couldn't even get a rise out of Dylan.

"I thought maybe you were avoiding me and Dara," Ted said.

"I didn't know you were coming for supper. And I took Lisa sailing because she's never been before," Dylan said, waiting for his brother to let them by. He glanced at Lisa, her hair a tousled mass of curls framing her face. She had taken off her hat and her cheeks had been kissed by the sun. She looked adorable and he had to resist the urge to kiss her again.

"Mom was getting ready to call up the Coast Guard." Ted stood aside to let them by.

"She knew where I was," Dylan said easily.

Stephanie stood with her back to them, wiping the table, when they entered the kitchen, Dara was loading the dishwasher and Erika was leaning on the counter chatting on the phone.

Alex looked up from the newspaper he was reading at the table and smiled at Lisa, then Dylan.

Dylan held his glance a moment, his mind sifting back to what he and Lisa had talked about. He wished he could understand exactly what his father was doing. He wished he could simply, as Lisa suggested, trust his own father.

Stephanie, catching the direction of Alex's gaze, looked over her shoulder, then straightened, her hand on her chest. "There you two are. What happened?"

Dylan shrugged away her concern, though he couldn't ignore the guilt her worried face gave him. "Lost track of time," he said, bending to kiss her on the cheek.

"My Dylan? Losing track of time?" Stephanie held his shoulder with one hand and gave him a long, hard look. She looked over at Lisa as if for confirmation of what she had just heard.

"Our brother, transforming into a human being right in front of our eyes," Ted said, dropping into a chair beside his father.

"Hey, Dylan." Amber came up behind him,

grabbed Dylan and spun him around. "Where were you? We were getting worried. You're never late."

"Lisa and I went sailing," he said, flicking his little sister under her chin.

Amber blinked. Threw a puzzled glance at Lisa. "In the middle of the day?"

Dylan shook his head at his family's unsubtle bewilderment. They made him sound positively neurotic.

"Did you two have supper? I've some left," Stephanie said, flipping her hand in the direction of the kitchen. "Ted and Dara were coming over, so I had lots."

"Thanks, Mom, but we grabbed a burger at a drive-through on the way home."

"Burgers? My goodness, you must have been hungry," Dara said.

"Some people like burgers," Ted said, glancing at his wife.

Dara turned away, her shoulders stiff. The tension between Dara and Ted was palpable, making Dylan thankful he and Lisa had missed supper.

"Hey, Dylan, Erika and I are going to a movie. We're leaving in half an hour," Amber said. "Do you wanna come?"

Thankful for the diversion, Dylan turned to Lisa. What better way to finish off a perfect day than by spending it in a darkened movie theater with Lisa? Even if he had to do it with his little sisters.

"What do you think, Lisa? Are you up to a movie?"

Her glance darted to Dara, then back to him. "I…I

don't know. I, uh, was thinking I might go out on my own.''

He frowned at her, puzzled at the change in her demeanor. All the way home she had been a laughing, pleasant companion alternately serious and teasing, never at a loss for words. But since Ted had met them at the door she had said absolutely nothing.

''Sure. I could bring you wherever you want to go.''

''No…no…it's okay. I'd like to go by myself.''

Her hesitant speech was nothing like the laughing, confident girl he had spent the day with. What was going on? ''Are you sure? I don't mind driving you.''

''Goodness, Dylan. Let the girl be. I doubt she's spent more than a minute away from any Mathesons since she got here,'' Ted said with a forced laugh.

Dylan threw him a warning glance, peeved both with his brother's interference and Lisa's sudden change.

But Ted's words reminded him of the rehearsal party. Lisa had elected to stay home then, as well, and when he'd come back early, she'd appeared to be just coming back from somewhere. And had acted just as unsettled.

Lisa toyed with her hat, her eyes avoiding his. ''I better get going,'' she said quietly.

Fifteen minutes later Dylan stood by the window of the study, watching Lisa get into a cab and leave. Dylan propped his shoulder against the window, pondering the puzzle of Lisa. Just before she left he'd overheard her talking to someone on her cell phone in her bedroom and she hadn't sounded happy.

The kisses they'd shared this afternoon had been surprising and had created a need to know more about her. So on the way home he had tried to draw more out of her. Her past life. What she did for fun. How she spent her time.

And while she was fun and witty and chatty, what he had found out could be written on a postage stamp.

Dylan pushed himself away from the window, his thoughts an unorganized chatter. He wanted their relationship to change. To deepen. This afternoon was a movement in that direction.

But where was it going?

He was leaving as soon as he was finished here. And when they got to Toronto, they would be going their separate ways.

They didn't have to.

He allowed the thought to settle. Played with it. He knew that compared to any other girl he had ever dated, she was by far the one he felt the closest to. The one who filled a need in him that others didn't.

But there were questions surrounding her that needed answering before they moved on. And she didn't seem willing to answer them.

With a light sigh he walked past her computer, glancing down as he did so. His eye caught the crumpled invoice lying beside it. When he had given it to her this morning he'd been quite sure there were two pieces of paper stuck together. But Lisa had said it was only a single invoice.

He picked it up, looking at it more closely. The invoice was white, but it had bits of yellow paper still clinging to it. He was right. There had been another paper.

He flipped through the file, but found no similarly stained memo. In fact, he found no yellow paper at all.

So where was it?

Dylan closed the file, impatiently tapping his fingers on the green folder. Why had she lied to him about it?

And where was she going right now?

Frustration battled with weariness. His father had asked Dylan to come and sort the business out but wasn't helping him. The woman he was growing more and more attracted to was becoming more and more of a mystery.

What was he doing here anyway?

"So what does this mean?" Lisa laid the memo carefully down on Gabe's table, her heartbeat pushing heavily against her ribs.

Gabe read the memo and clutched the back of his head with his hands. "Where did you get that?"

"It was stuck inside an invoice that was stuck to the outside of a file. I'm guessing Dylan and I weren't supposed to see it." Lisa leaned forward, resting her elbows on the table. "What couldn't you do anymore, Gabe? What did you neglect to tell me?"

"Did you show that to anyone?" He spoke without any of his previous bluster.

"No. I had to lie to Dylan about it. I hid it in my bedroom." Lisa cringed inwardly as she thought once again of the subterfuge she'd had to practice to get the memo to Gabe without Dylan's knowledge. It hurt to think of the puzzled look on his face this evening when she had said she wanted to go out.

She had never been very good at lying. And after the two kisses they'd shared, her duplicity bothered her even more.

Gabe leaned his head against the window, rolling his forehead back and forth. "Have you gotten into the files in the office?"

"No. Dylan and I spent the day sailing. Dara was gone and Alex didn't think we should go looking without her around."

Gabe hit the window with his fist and spun around. "I thought I threw that memo away."

"You didn't answer my question, Gabe. What does it mean?"

Gabe fell into the chair across from her, looking defeated. "You have to promise to just listen, okay?"

"Listen to what?" Her impatience made her short-tempered. "You haven't said anything worthwhile yet."

"Just listen." He held his hand up in warning. He tunneled his hands through his hair, clutching his skull. "Remember how when I first came to Vancouver, I had trouble finding a job? So I was running out of money and I met some guy."

Lisa sat back, clutching her midriff with her arms, an all too familiar tingle of dread beginning in her stomach. She bit back her anger and listened as Gabe had asked her to.

Gabe quietly related a story that echoed ones she had heard before. The wrong crowd. Questionable activities. A brush with the law.

"Lucky for me, they couldn't pin anything on me because I wasn't really involved. Just along for the ride. So I got off. No criminal record. Nothing. I made a deal with God that I would never do that stuff again. Then I met a girl. A nice girl. She worked for Matheson Telecom. Told me they were looking for an accountant. So I applied and got the job." Gabe stopped here, tapping his thumbs together. He gave Lisa a wavering smile. "Needless to say, I didn't make any mention of my little adventure. Things were going really well. Then one day I found a set of duplicate invoices. One was for less than the other. I wasn't supposed to see them both. I asked Dara and she sat me down and told me if I didn't keep my mouth shut I would get fired. She said she had asked around, had talked to that girl. She said she knew about my activities and that I had lied on my application about any involvement with the law." Gabe closed his eyes and rubbed his forehead with his forefinger. Just as he used to when he was a little boy. "And I had. But what could I do, Lisa? Nothing came of it. Nothing happened. Next thing I know she was getting me to do just the work on her father's company. They're customers of Matheson Telecom. It looked a little fishy to me and when I asked her about it, she said to mind my own business. Then there was talk around the office of missing money. I got scared, wrote the memo and got fired.''

''Why didn't you tell me this right away?'' The dread in Lisa's stomach grew with each word her brother uttered. ''Why didn't you go to Alex?''

Gabe shook his head. ''And tell him what? That I lied on my job application? Tell him that I thought his daughter-in-law was cheating him?''

Lisa thought of her own job application and her own evasions. She could hardly call Gabe out for that when she wasn't innocent, either.

''Did you do anything wrong, Gabe?''

He looked away. ''I did what I was told until I realized it was stupid to be manipulated like that.''

Dread clutched Lisa with chilly fingers. ''Did you take any money, Gabe?''

Gabe's gaze flew to hers. ''Not a penny. That's why you have to get into my computer. That will let you know if anything's been done on it. It's the only way she could have moved stuff around.'' Gabe held Lisa's gaze. ''Didn't you go to the office this afternoon?''

Lisa pushed back a beat of guilt. ''No, I told you— Dara wasn't in and Alex wouldn't let us access the files without her being around.''

''I'll give you my password to get into my computer. If it's still there.'' He pulled out a piece of paper and wrote something down on it. ''This is it. You don't have much time, you know.''

Lisa knew that far too well. Each day she spent with Dylan brought them closer to the end of their time here. And each visit to Gabe created a combination of subterfuge and fear of being found out.

She glanced at her watch. She didn't dare stay away too much longer.

"I better go," Lisa said, getting up. She leaned over her brother and dropped a light kiss on his head. "You take care. I'm going to see if we can get into the office soon. Love you."

Gabe caught her by the hand. "I never tell you often enough, do I? How much you help me?"

Lisa smiled down at him, her heart overflowing with love. "I think I know," she said softly, absently brushing a strand of hair away from his forehead, just as she used to do when he was younger. "I have to help you. You're all I've got."

"Now Dylan's got himself a girl,
"And she's a pretty thing."

Erika and Amber stood on a stage at the front of the hall decorated with balloons and ribbons in honor of Alex and Stephanie's anniversary. Laughter swept over the large group of people seated at tables as the twins looked up from the crumpled paper they held between them.

"We hope that this one sticks around
"Long enough to get a..."

Erika paused, her grin mischievous.

"Raise," she said.

"That doesn't rhyme," someone called out from the crowd.

"Neither does stock option," Amber said, singling

Dylan out with her smile. "And that was our only other choice."

Lisa glanced sidelong at Dylan, wondering how he took this bantering. But Dylan was sitting back in his chair, his tie loosened, his hands folded over his stomach, laughing as hard as anyone else.

Amber sent a wink in Lisa's direction. "Thanks, Lisa, for daring to show up to yet another Matheson family function, Mom and Dad's anniversary. You deserve a medal."

"She deserves our sympathy," Ted called out in an overloud voice from another corner of the hall.

Lisa couldn't stop the blush that reddened her cheeks at the implications in the comments. Nor could she stop the surge of guilt at the deception she and Dylan were playing out.

And the deception she herself was playing out on a family that had accepted her with open arms and an open heart.

She endured an instant of pain, intense and familiar, remembering the many times she and Gabe had stood in the hallway of a new home, wondering how they were going to fit in. The Mathesons had taken in Dylan's unknown girlfriend with grace and aplomb and love. Even the twins had accepted her and had offered clothing and makeup and little inside jokes and stories about Dylan that made him both more endearing and kind.

And now she was sitting through this evening watching skits and hearing poems that portrayed family life in the Matheson household. Listening to remembrances that showed what a close and loving family they were.

The twins' poem moved on to the other family members and they finished to a round of applause. They sketched a quick bow and winked at Lisa.

"Mom and Dad want to say a few words now, to end the evening." The twins gestured toward their parents, who got up from their seats at the head table and made their way to the stage, holding hands as they often did.

Alex tapped on the microphone and looked around the room with a huge smile.

"We are so thankful that all of you could come here. And we're especially thankful for all the work Erika, Amber, Ted, Dara and Tiffany did. We're thankful Dylan and Lisa could come from so far away."

Lisa tried not to squirm at the pairing of her name with Dylan's. Just as if they were a real couple.

"We're thankful Chelsea and Jordan were willing to accommodate our anniversary around their honeymoon."

Huge cheers went up for the newly married couple.

"This evening has been a blessing to Stephanie and me." Alex glanced sidelong at his wife and they shared a look of love so deep it made Lisa smile just to see it. "But with our thanks, we want to thank our Lord for His enduring love. His blessings through good and bad times. What we have on this earth is less important to us than who we are. And in everything we've done, Stephanie and I have hoped and prayed that we have shown our children that. Thank you all for coming. There's lots of food yet. The party's not over until the last Matheson is gone. Have a good evening yet.''

Glasses were tinkled all around the hall signaling a request for a kiss, and Alex and Stephanie graciously responded. Their kiss was discreet but warm. Another cheer went up, and with a quick wave Alex and Stephanie returned to their seats.

A wave of voices rose around them. But Lisa couldn't look at Dylan. Couldn't talk to him. Instead, in an attempt to pretend busyness, she toyed with the silvery hearts sprinkled on the heavy damask tablecloth, while her heart grew heavier and heavier. Each day she and Dylan spent together brought them closer to the end of this time together. She felt an urgency that no longer was attached only to finding out what she could for Gabe. Now her urgency had as much or more to do with Dylan.

Sooner or later she had to tell Dylan who she really was. Which would mean she would not return to Toronto with him.

And that would be the end of the dream.

''Excuse me,'' she murmured to Dylan and the people sitting at their table. She got up and walked outside, feeling suddenly claustrophobic. Once outside, she took a deep breath of the blessedly cool air. She leaned her elbows on the railing of the balcony, watching how the gold lights of the downtown buildings of Vancouver spangled the water across the bay. Under other circumstances she would have been entranced. But tonight guilt weighed heavily on her heart.

Lord, what have I started? Lord, what do I do? How do I get myself out of this? I am starting to care for this man. And care for his family.

"Hey, are you okay?" Dylan came up behind her, resting his hand on her shoulder.

"Just wanted to get a breath of fresh air," Lisa said, staying where she was.

"It was getting a bit close in there, wasn't it?" Dylan's fingers lightly stroked her shoulder. "I hope you weren't too embarrassed with the girls' poem?"

Lisa spun around, holding his gaze. "I don't know what I felt." She wished she could be more articulate. More honest.

"I know what I did." Dylan's eyes glittered in the reflected light and his expression grew serious. He ran his finger along the side of her face. "Lisa, something is happening between us. I know you feel it, too."

Lisa wanted him to stop, but his words soothed the ache of yearning that had been growing since she met him. Just a few more moments, she thought, closing her eyes and her mind to the second thoughts that clamored for attention. Just a few more memories.

He held her shoulders and drew her close to him, his breath sighing through her hair. "Let's get away from here." He took her hand and led her along the balcony to a set of stone steps that led to a discreetly lit garden.

The grass was damp from the shower this afternoon, but Lisa didn't mind. She was glad to get away from the party and be where she wanted most to be right now.

Alone with Dylan.

They followed the edge of the manicured lawn, staying close to the flower gardens that sent out a heady mixture of scents. They followed a path to a gazebo, and Lisa's heart quickened when she saw it was empty.

Their footfalls echoed on the wooden floor, and when they were under the roof, Dylan turned to Lisa and drew her into his arms.

Lisa swallowed, sent up a prayer for strength, then leaned back.

"Dylan, I'm starting to feel so guilty about what we're doing to your family," she said, pressing her hands against his chest. "Every day I feel like more and more of a fraud. I don't know how long I can do this anymore. Your family is so great and they are acting like I really am your girlfriend." She stopped, the word catching in her throat. "And I really like them."

Dylan drew back, a light frown pulling his dark eyebrows together. "What are you saying?"

Lisa looked straight ahead, focusing on his loosened tie. "I think we should tell them the truth."

"And what is the truth?" Dylan lifted her face with his finger, smiling down at her. "That we don't like each other? That what happened on the sailboat was just an act? That what is happening now is staged for the benefit of my family?" He cupped her chin with his hand, his eyes intent on hers. "I don't think that's the truth, either. Not anymore."

At her center unvoiced and uncertain feelings swirled as she grasped at the meaning of his words. Did she dare hope that they might have a future?

She drifted toward him, drawn by the emotion in his voice, by her own uncertain and changing emotions.

She laid her hand on his chest, as if forestalling the inevitable, trying to find some solid ground on which to make a stand.

Lisa swallowed as he lowered his head to hers. She stopped him, her emotions seesawing between her changing feelings for him and the precariousness of her situation.

She had to tell him.

She couldn't tell him. Because if she did, everything she had right now would be lost.

"But I'm not a girlfriend, am I?" She didn't want an answer, but she had to speak the words aloud.

Dylan shrugged, still holding her. "I think you are. I think I feel more for you than I've felt for any so-called girlfriend I've ever had."

His words wrapped themselves around her, teasing, alluring. And dangerous.

"You know what your problem is, Lisa?" Dylan asked, his hands clasped at her waist. "You think too much."

"First time I've ever been accused of that," Lisa said with a light laugh.

Dylan smiled back. "I think we have a future, Lisa. I really do."

Lisa closed her eyes as he lowered his head. His kiss was gentle, sweet.

And heartbreaking.

"Okay, I figured I'd find you two out here."

Like a clumsy hand sweeping away a spiderweb, Ted's slurred voice whisked away the beautiful and fragile moment. Lisa dropped her hand and sucked in a deep breath, willing her heart to quit pounding.

"You two look pretty cozy," Ted said, coming into the gazebo. He swayed a little, as if he'd been drinking. "I do b'lieve this is the first time I've ever seen you with your arm around a girl."

Ted turned to Lisa, his eyes glazed. "Did you know that your boyfriend schedules his dates on his handheld computer?" He nodded slowly. "Just marks them in along with business meetings and reminders to pick up his dry cleaning."

Lisa heard Dylan sigh and she glanced sidelong at him. He crossed his arms over his chest, looking slightly bored. "And why do you think Lisa would want to know that?"

Ted rocked a little, grinning. "So she knows what she's in for." Ted glanced over at Lisa. "Course, how many boyfriends make their girlfriends work on their holiday? Huh? But that's our Dylan. He's found the ultimate girlfriend. A secretary. That's my brother. Always efficient."

Lisa felt a pang of hurt that shouldn't have bothered her. She *was* Dylan's secretary, in spite of the whispered promise she had heard only moments ago. In spite of feelings that were changing.

"Lisa is more than a secretary, and you know that,

Ted,'' Dylan said, pulling Lisa even closer. Lisa clung to him, drawing from his strength.

''So why do you have her helping you? You come sweeping in here—'' Ted waved a feeble hand in Lisa's direction ''—with your secretary. Come to fix everything. Maybe even my job.''

''You know I don't want your job, Ted. I'm quitting the company. The last thing I want to do is sweep in and take over.''

''So why are you hanging around here, poking your nose into the books?''

''Because Dad asked me to.''

''Did you find what you're looking for?''

Lisa watched Ted, listened to the bravado in his voice. And she wondered how much he knew about Gabe and Dara.

''If we could get into the office, I'm sure we would find more than what we've been finding by only looking through the files Dara has given us,'' Lisa blurted out.

She clamped her lips together as Ted's swivering gaze landed on her. What had made her blurt that out and draw attention to herself?

''Really? And how would you know what to look for, Miss secretary slash girlfriend?''

''I think you've said enough, Ted,'' Dylan said, annoyance edging his voice.

Ted shook his head slowly. Laughed a humorless laugh. ''Haven't said enough, really. Never say enough.'' He took a step closer to Lisa. She could smell the liquor on his breath. ''Let me warn you, Lisa. My brother? Cold. No fun. Busy, busy, busy.

Such a hard worker." He swayed a moment and Dylan grabbed him. "Dara didn't love him. Said she couldn't."

Dylan's eyes were narrowed, his lips thin. "You better go back, Ted. We didn't invite you here, and Lisa doesn't want to hear what you have to say."

"I think she does." Ted laid a hand on Lisa's shoulder. "Did you know your Dylan used to date my wife? But she didn't want a cold fish like him. She only wanted me. Just me."

Lisa felt a surprising flash of jealousy. But as she looked more closely at Ted, beyond the anger that clenched his jaw, she saw pain in his eyes. And she heard the uncertainty in his voice.

"Then it's a good thing she married you, isn't it?" Lisa said quietly, feeling suddenly sorry for him.

"Let go of her, Ted," Dylan warned, taking a step nearer his brother.

Lisa gently shook her head in warning at Dylan. She sensed that Ted wasn't a threat. "I'm sure she still cares for you."

Ted blinked, as if trying to absorb what she'd said. He let go of Lisa's shoulder and looked past her, his bluster and bravado slipping away like clothes off a hanger. "I don't know anymore." Ted sank onto a bench lining the gazebo, his hands holding his head. "I don't know if she loves me anymore." His words were slurred. Almost as if he was crying.

"Why shouldn't she, Ted?" Lisa asked.

"She doesn't talk to me anymore. Full of secrets." He rubbed his hands over his head again and again.

Lisa felt her heart quicken. Maybe Ted knew something after all. "What secrets, Ted?"

Ted looked up at her, his bleary eyes blinking as if trying to focus on her. "That's why they're secrets. I dunno about them."

"Lisa, don't bother trying to talk to him now. He's had too much to drink." Dylan tugged on Lisa's arm.

Lisa glanced back at Ted, feeling torn.

Ted needs to know.

Lisa wondered what he knew. And wondered, if Dylan talked to him, if Ted would let it out.

She didn't stop to examine her motives. Lisa ran to his side and caught Dylan by the arm, stopping him. "I think he needs to talk to you, Dylan," she whispered. "Listen to him."

Dylan clenched his jaw, staring at Ted, who still sat hunched over, then looked down at Lisa, his features softening. "Why should I talk to him now?"

"Because he's your brother." And because he might be able to help my brother.

"Ted has never needed anyone. He's only used people."

"Well, he needs you now." Lisa tugged lightly. "Please talk to him."

"Why does this matter so much to you?" Dylan touched Lisa's cheek lightly, smiling now.

A week ago it would have been solely because of Gabe. But now…

"Family is a gift from God," she said softly, her words sincere. "And I think this is a chance to fix a few things in yours."

Dylan's expression grew serious. "You really believe that, don't you?"

"I do. Don't waste this opportunity."

Dylan shook his head, but he let Lisa lead him back to Ted's side. He hunkered down beside his brother. "Ted, what's wrong?"

Ted ran his fingers through his neatly combed hair again and again, still looking down. "I don't think Dara loves me anymore."

"Why do you say that?" Dylan asked, his own voice quieter.

Ted looked up at Dylan. "She never talks to me anymore. She's always so busy. All she talks about is you and Lisa."

"What do you mean?"

Ted slowly shook his head. "She's tired of having to run files around for nothing. She doesn't have time. When she's home all she does is say how she wishes your dad would stop putting pressure on her to cooperate."

"What do you want me to do, Ted?"

"This is a waste of time," Ted said. "Tell Dad to stop pokin' around. It's all Dara can talk about. We found out who did it. Just let it go. Please. She's scared Dad's trying to find a way to get me out and put you in."

"Okay, Ted. I'll talk to Dad. We're not getting anywhere on it anyhow."

Lisa stifled a flare of panic at Dylan's assurances. Ted was supposed to confirm her suspicions. Help her clear Gabe. This was not what was supposed to happen. What had she done?

Dylan pushed himself to his feet and caught Ted by the hand. "Don't worry about this anymore. It will be over soon."

Lisa closed her eyes. *Dear Lord, this wasn't supposed to be the outcome.*

What was she going to do now?

Chapter Ten

She couldn't sleep anymore. What she had done last night flipped and spun through her mind, keeping her awake.

She should have shown Dylan the memo right away before her emotions for this family interfered with her plans. But if she gave Dylan the memo now, he would wonder why she had kept it from him.

With an exasperated sigh she tossed off the blankets, wrapped her robe around her. She pulled the offending piece of paper from a drawer in her room and left.

She drifted down the stairs, making her way to the study.

The door was half-open and she quietly slipped through it. The early-morning light was already creeping in. She hesitated a moment, glancing over her shoulder, then strode to Dylan's desk, opened the file folder on the top and laid the memo inside, letting part of it show above the file folder's edge.

As she closed the folder she felt a tick of relief. Maybe it would make the difference. And maybe it would incriminate her.

Either way, time was winding down. She couldn't help Gabe anymore. Her fantasy with Dylan was coming to an end in spite of his whispered promises.

Dylan would return to Toronto, and then he would leave Matheson Telecom for his new job.

Pain, hard and sharp, surged through her at the thought of him leaving. She couldn't stop it and she couldn't change it. And she couldn't go back to Toronto with him.

She looked around and saw the shelf that held the Bible. With a cry of sorrow she stumbled toward it like a lost person seeking home.

She snatched it off the shelf and held it close.

What do you hope to find here?

Panic clutched at her as the conversation she and Dylan had had with Ted spun up once more. Dylan was going to stop looking. Gabe was still seen as guilty. What was going to happen to him if she quit now? She knew from experience that if things didn't get resolved she didn't know what Gabe would do.

But how could she convince Dylan to keep digging without letting him know who she was?

She couldn't tell him. Not yet.

With a tired sigh she dropped into the large leather sofa facing the fireplace. She tucked her feet under her and snapped on the light, creating an intimate cone of luminance in the darkened study.

She paged through the Bible, her previous question nagging at her. Did she want answers to her dilemma? A solution to the problems she had taken on?

Was she hoping to recapture the connection she'd felt so strongly in church?

She paged past the prophets to the New Testament, the Bible opening to the book of Peter. Her eyes skimmed the words, then stopped.

"God opposes the proud, but gives grace to the humble. Humble yourselves therefore under God's mighty hand that He may lift you up in due time. Cast all your anxiety on Him because He cares for you."

Lisa read the words again. And again. They pressed against her, exposing her even as they gave her comfort. She knew that she had to let go of her plans, yet if she did what would happen to Gabe? To her?

For the past few days she had allowed herself a fantasy. That Dylan really was her boyfriend and she was a part of this family. That together they would prove Gabe innocent.

But it wasn't going to happen once Dylan and his family heard the truth from her. And even if she didn't tell them, Dylan was leaving the company. Would she go back to Toronto and pursue the faint hope Dylan had held out to her in his whispered promises last night? Would those promises still hold once he found out she had lied to him?

Please, Lord. Just a little while longer, she prayed as the loneliness of the past few years and the sacrifices she had made for Gabe in her personal life nagged at her resolve. *Let me hold on to this dream just a little more?*

But even as the prayer formulated in her mind, she knew God wouldn't answer it. She knew what she had to do. She closed the Bible and set it aside. *Cast all your anxiety on Him because He cares for you.*

Lisa pressed her hands against her face, her emotions warring with truth. *Help me, Lord. Help me find the right time.*

The door to the study creaked open and Lisa whirled around, her hand on her chest.

It was Dylan. His hair was still tousled from sleep and whiskers darkened his cheeks. He wore a loose T-shirt and blue jeans. And he looked even better than he had last night in a suit and tie.

"Hey, there," he said, his voice still sleep roughened. "You couldn't sleep, either?"

Lisa shook her head, her heart throbbing in her chest in a confused combination of fear and anticipation.

Dylan walked into the study and stopped by the end table beside Lisa's chair. "When I saw the light under the door, I thought you were my mother. She sometimes comes in here early in the morning and has her devotions."

"I'm…I'm…sorry. I'll leave." Lisa struggled to untangle her feet from her long robe to stand, but Dylan caught her by the shoulder and eased her down.

"It's okay. She doesn't do it every morning." Dylan came around the couch and hunkered down in front of her. He caught her by the hands, toying gently with her fingers as he smiled up at her. "I was thinking about you this morning."

In spite of her resolve, a soft yearning grew within her at his touch, at the intimacy of his lowered voice. Giving in to an impulse, she reached out and feathered his hair back from his forehead, letting her fingers trail down the rough stubble of his cheek.

"I was thinking about you, too." The words slipped past her defenses. She fought back the reality of their situation, deferring the moment when she was going to tell him the truth.

"So why couldn't you sleep?" Dylan lifted her fingers to his lips and kissed them lightly, his eyes on hers.

His soft question coupled with the touch of his mouth roused an agitation of feelings within her.

Tell him. Tell him now.

No. Not yet. This is too precious.

Lisa held his eyes as she swallowed hard against the shame she could feel pushing its way up her throat.

You promised you would at the right moment.

But she couldn't. Not with Dylan so close. So dear.

She knew what was happening. Somehow, in the process of trying to save her brother, she had lost her heart. And when Dylan leaned closer and touched his lips to her cheek, she knew she was going to wait.

"I didn't think I'd ever find anyone like you," he said quietly, pushing her aside so he could sit beside her. "It sounds corny, but you make me feel whole."

He sighed, still holding her hand as he angled his chin toward the Bible. "Were you reading it?"

"I was. I feel like I need to connect. To find peace." Her words trailed off as the contradiction of what she had been reading and what she should do warred within her.

Dylan reached past her and pulled the Bible off the table. "What were you reading?"

"First Peter. 'Cast all your anxieties on him.'" Lisa laughed lightly, trying to dispel the heaviness that had crept over them. "Easier to read about than do."

"Do you have a favorite passage?" Dylan leafed through the Bible, angling her a smile as he did so.

"First Corinthians 13."

"Ah. The love passage." Dylan flipped through the Bible and found it. "'If I speak in the tongues of men and of angels, but have not love, I am only a resounding gong or a clanging cymbal,'" he read, his voice growing quiet. Reverent. "'Love is patient, love is kind. It does not envy, it does not boast, it is not proud.'" Dylan paused there, his finger resting on the passage. "That covers quite a lot of territory, doesn't it?"

"It also makes love so much more than a simple word."

"Loving someone can be the hardest thing to do," Dylan said, setting the Bible aside. "It's not always a soft, mushy emotion."

Lisa leaned back against the buttery leather of the couch, her eyes on Dylan as a surprising peace drifted over her. She kept quiet as she thought about what he had read. About love.

God's love.

Her love.

She let the word slip through her mind, drifting, incomplete. She loved her brother. She loved her parents.

But what she felt for Dylan was something completely different. And she felt the stirring of a newer, even more frightening emotion. She glanced at Dylan quietly leafing through the Bible. He looked up at her.

Like ice water flowing through her veins the realization dawned. She loved him.

She couldn't. It was too soon. Too sudden.

Yet even as her thoughts negated it, her heart told her it was true. Dylan was exactly the kind of man she had been looking for.

Why had she found him now? And under these circumstances?

The door behind them swept open and light poured out of the ceiling fixture.

"Oh, I'm sorry," Stephanie said, standing in the doorway. "I didn't know you were here."

"I'm just leaving…right now," Lisa said softly. "I need to have a shower." She gave Dylan a sad smile, then left, wishing she could outrun what she had just discovered.

"Dylan, I'm sorry. Was I interrupting something?"

Dylan smiled. "Believe it or not, I was reading to her out of the Bible."

"The Bible?" Stephanie's voice betrayed her confusion. She tightened the sash on her red silk robe, glancing over her shoulder as if seeking confirmation.

"Yes. First Corinthians 13, if you must know."

"Dylan. That's..." Dylan felt his mother's hand on his shoulder. Heard the wonder in her voice. A wonder that echoed his own. "You don't know how I've prayed that you would find someone who would share..." She stopped again, emotion stopping her.

Dylan stood, turning to Stephanie, and saw the glisten of tears in her eyes. He gave his mother a gentle smile.

"She's a wonderful girl, Dylan. I sense that she's seeking the Lord."

Dylan looked past his mother at the open door of the study. In spite of the tender moment they had shared, he still felt as if a part of Lisa was evading him. As if there were things about her he didn't know. "I wish I knew exactly what she was seeking."

Stephanie took him by the arm and pulled him onto the couch Lisa had just left so suddenly. "You just have to be patient, Dylan. Something you're not very good at as a rule."

"Thanks for the vote of confidence, Mom," Dylan said, suppressing a sigh.

"In all other respects you are an amazing, wonderful person and any girl would be lucky to have you." Stephanie gave his captured arm a shake as if to get his full attention.

"So why do I get the feeling I don't know her very well?"

"You've only been together a short while," Stephanie said quietly.

"Yet I really care about her," he reluctantly admitted, knowing what chain of events his confession would create. His mother would tell the girls and they would be all over him like a bad suit giving advice on dating and the best place to go looking for engagement rings.

"Dylan, I'm so happy. Your father and I have prayed so long that you would find someone to care about. Someone who could share your faith."

Dylan held his mother's longing gaze, his own doubts coming to the fore. "I don't know if we share that, Mother. A faith."

"She came to church with you. You were just reading out of the Bible together."

Dylan leaned back, sinking into the cool leather of the couch, feeling inadequate in the face of his mother's conviction. "Don't give me too much credit, Mom. I haven't done either for a long time."

"But you're doing it now." Stephanie stroked Dylan's hair back from his face much as she had when he was younger. "And God acknowledges each small step you make. 'A bruised reed He will not break, a smouldering wick He will not quench.'"

Dylan laid his head back, suddenly tired. "That's exactly how I feel. Like a bruised reed. Not enough life to stand, but not completely bent over yet."

"In your faith life?"

"And my personal life. And my professional life."
Except with Lisa. With her he felt fully alive. Strong.

"You're still angry with your father about Ted,
aren't you?" Stephanie's voice was quiet, but her
pain and sorrow poured through her words. "I was
hoping this week together would remove some of
that. I was hoping you would change your mind
about leaving and stay with the company."

"It's too late for that, Mom." Dylan sighed, pressing his forefinger to his temple. The holiday had appeared endless before they left, but it had flown on
wings. Now, as the end neared, he wished for more
time. "As for Dad, I'm not as angry as I was. Especially not after listening to poor Ted last night."
Dylan tilted his head toward his mother, the couch
sighing with the movement. "He's far unhappier
with Dad's decision than I ever was, Mom."

"I know."

The simple admission caught him unawares.

"So does your father," Stephanie continued, slipping the silky ends of her robe's sash through her
fingers.

Dylan glanced out the window of the study. From
where he sat he could just see the early-morning sunlight glinting gold off the office buildings of downtown. Morning in the city.

He used to love coming early to his office and
watching the sun come up, wondering what the new
day was going to bring.

But for the past few years all that morning had
brought was a sense that he was simply marking
time. His work in Toronto didn't challenge him and

didn't give him enough control to make any decisions that would take the company in dramatic new directions. Though he had done well in the branch office, the real authority still came from Vancouver.

"So why does he allow Ted to simply flounder on?" Dylan asked.

"You're not the only proud person in this family, Dylan. It's hard for your father to admit he's made a mistake. Just as it's hard for Ted to admit he can't do the job. Just as it's hard for you to simply tell your father that you should be in charge of the company, not Ted. And now that you're quitting the company…"

"I'm not going to wait anymore."

Stephanie swung around to face him, leaning close to him, her eyes flashing, her jaw set. "No. Instead you're going to run away. And you're wrong about your father. He's not as driven as you. And he's much softer. I love him for it, but when it comes to the business, Matheson Telecom needs someone like you."

Her anger washed over him, surprising in its intensity. His mother was usually all softness and gentleness. He listened.

"Your father needs you to confront him and tell him that enough is enough. If you want to be in charge, then tell him that. If you do, you will give Alex and Ted an easy out. Like I said, in their own way they have pride, as well." Stephanie brushed a hand over her forehead, as if brushing away her anger. "You're the only one I can talk to right now, Dylan. Ted has his own problems, and your father has his own secrets…." Her voice faltered and as quickly as the movement of clouds across the sun, her anger faded away. "I don't know what's going on anymore. I only know that since that accountant Gabe was fired things have gone all haywire in this house. Right now you and Lisa and the twins are the only people in this house who don't have any secrets."

But Lisa did have her own secrets.

"I want this family whole again, Dylan. I want things the way they're supposed to be in a family that confesses to love the Lord."

"And I'm supposed to be the one to do it, Mom?" Dylan asked quietly. "What if I don't even know myself about my relationship with the Lord?"

"God never forgets you, Dylan. He never lets go. You have been a child of God since you were born and I cling to that promise every day." Stephanie caught his hand and held it between her own. "Every day your father and I pray for you and for all our children. We have prayed that you would find a relationship with God."

The words gave him comfort. Strength.

He turned his mother's hand over, tracing the raised veins in the backs of her hands as he used to as a child. "I haven't prayed for a while, Mom. I don't know how to start."

"Do you want to?" Stephanie's voice was a soft whisper, as if she hardly dared voice her request too loud.

Dylan nodded.

"Okay. You start with something simple and I'll pray it for you. We'll keep going like that."

Dylan bent his head, pushing aside the voices that had lured him away all these years. The voices that told him God was for women and weak men. The thoughts that fooled him into thinking that he could be strong on his own.

With his mother beside him, he dug down to the bedrock of his faith. To the God he had known as a child.

"Dear Lord," he prayed, "I don't know where to start. I only know that I want to know You more."

Stephanie responded, adding her own prayer. And as her voice lilted through familiar cadences, her sincerity pouring through in the touch of her hands on his, in the feeling in her voice, Dylan felt his unraveling ends slowly becoming whole.

And he let God into his life again.

Lisa sat at her computer desk, her mind a storm of thoughts and emotions.

Since her epiphany in this very same place this morning, she couldn't find a place in her mind that brought her serenity.

She knew only the truth would. But the truth was a double-edged sword. It would bring her peace, but it would also sever any hopes of a continuing relationship with Dylan.

She turned back to the crumpled invoice lying beside her computer. Dylan didn't want to look anymore, but she couldn't quit. Though she loved Dylan, she had made a promise to herself to help her brother. And she had to go through with that. No matter what the cost.

She had pulled the invoice out of the file and was looking at it again, sensing that it held more than just a hiding place for the memo.

She booted up her computer and punched in the date of the invoice. A list of other invoices came up, but not this one. Why had Dara not entered it?

An invoice with the same date for the same company came up. But for a different amount.

She frowned at the invoice, wondering what she was supposed to be seeing. She realized she had taken the wrong piece of paper to Gabe's. Instead of the memo, she should have taken this invoice.

"I didn't think I'd find you in here anymore."

Dylan's voice swept over Lisa's swirling thoughts, bringing love and helpless yearning in its wake.

She turned to him. How could she not?

He rested his hip against her desk, bringing him close enough that she could smell his aftershave. He had tidied up since she'd seen him last. "You seemed a little upset this morning. Are you okay now?"

His deep voice, coupled with his concern, rekindled her emotions. Created a faint hope she hardly dared nurture.

She looked away, quashing her feelings. "I'm okay." Which was a lie. She knew that no matter what happened to her in the future, she would not walk away without scars from this time spent with Dylan.

"Okay enough to come have breakfast with us?"

"There's a few things I want to finish up yet."
Besides, she had spent too much time with his family
already and she felt a need to get her relationship
with Dylan back to where it should be. Back to
where it was safe. If that could even happen.

"Don't you have the feeling we're missing something?" she asked, pushing aside her feelings.
"Something that's right under our noses?"

Dylan waggled his hand, as if considering. "I
don't know. Not that it matters. I told Ted we'd back
off, and Dad doesn't seem to be too involved."

"If your father wasn't, why would he ask you to
come here?" Lisa fought down her panic. Dylan had
to keep going. If they didn't find out the truth, she
was afraid of what would happen to her brother.
"Ted is the one asking you to quit, not your father."

Dylan shrugged. "I wish I knew what he wanted.
I need to sit down and have a heart-to-heart with him
before we go."

"You don't have much time," Lisa said quietly,
her concern shifting from her brother to Dylan. She
got the feeling that Alex cared about the problems in
the company, but that he also had his own agenda in
dealing with them.

The sharp ring of the phone made Lisa jump. Dylan ignored it.

"Shouldn't you get that?" she said.

He shook his head as he ran his finger lightly over
her cheek in an intimate gesture that made Lisa
quiver inside.

Dylan smiled a crooked smile. "My mother thinks

I should talk to my dad, as well. Are you two in cahoots?''

"No. But I like your parents. A lot.''

"And she likes you. A lot.'' He grew still, his eyes holding hers.

He's going to kiss me, Lisa thought, her heart skipping in her chest. I want him to.

I can't let him.

"Dylan, Dara's on the phone for you.'' Amber stuck her head in the study. "Says she has something important to tell you.''

Dylan blew out his breath and glanced back at his sister. "Thanks, Amber. I'll take it in here.'' He reached behind him and caught the phone off his desk, but didn't move from Lisa's side.

Lisa moved to get up, to give him privacy, but he gently laid his hand on her shoulder, forestalling her. As if negating Ted's comment about Dara and Dylan. Reassuring her he had nothing to hide.

"So, Dara. What can I do for you?'' Dylan smiled down at Lisa, his fingers lingering on her shoulder. His smile held, then faded.

"I'm glad to hear that, Dara,'' Dylan said. He nodded as if listening to more that she had to say, then slowly pulled his hand away from Lisa, frowning. "How did you manage to do that?... No, I hadn't heard anything about it... Are you sure that's where the money came from?... Of course I'll tell Dad.... Ted already knows.... Well, I guess that ties it all up. Thanks, Dara. This makes things a lot easier for everybody. Congratulations.'' Dylan pressed a button ending the phone call, then turned to Lisa. "Dara managed to get into Gabe's computer. She found the money that's been missing. So that officially ends our part of the job.''

Lisa stared at Dylan as his words slowly found their way to her mind. She tried to grab hold of them. Make them make sense. ''So where's the money? How did she manage to find it? Is she sure it's his?''

''She said she found it in an account he'd set up under a numbered company.'' Dylan pushed himself away from her desk. ''That makes the next step that much easier. We'll have to be pressing charges against that accountant now.''

''What do you mean press charges?''

''If the missing money is in his account, he's guilty.'' Dylan frowned at her. ''This isn't a problem, Lisa. This is a good thing. Now we can finally put this all behind us.'' He caught her by the hand and pulled her to her feet. ''Now we can focus on the really important things,'' he said with a grin.

Lisa couldn't look at him. Couldn't think. Her mind was a whirl of thoughts and confusion. She had seen Gabe just a few days ago. He hadn't said anything about money. He wasn't living as if he had any extra. Where could it have come from?

It was as if her heart had frozen, sending ice through her arteries.

Was Gabe guilty after all?

Dylan gave Lisa's hands a little shake, as if trying to catch her attention. ''Why so glum? It's over. No more digging into files. No more listening to evasions. We've only got one more day here. Let's spend it doing something fun.''

Fun? Lisa tried to gather her thoughts. Tried to put them in some kind of order. Gabe was innocent. She knew it. She had to believe it.

"How did Dara manage to find the money now?" she asked, refusing to give up on her brother so quickly. "According to your father it's been missing for a while now. How come she didn't find it any sooner?"

"Dara said it took her a while to hack in to Gabe's computer. She found evidence of a numbered company and a bank account in that name. The money was in that bank account."

"I don't know, Dylan," Lisa said, pulling her hands away from his, needing the distance to focus on what she had to say. "I don't have a good feeling about this. Seems to me that finding this money is too convenient. Why didn't she find it sooner? Why didn't Dara let us come and work in the office? There are just too many questions."

"What do you care, Lisa? All that's come of this is more work for yourself."

"I knew this was going to be a working holiday," Lisa said, struggling to find the right words to explain herself without looking guilty. "And I'm still your secretary." She lifted her hands in a gesture of surrender. "I just have the feeling that Dara is hiding something."

Dylan shrugged. "What?"

Lisa drew in a long, slow breath, willing her racing heart to slow down. Much depended on how she handled this.

She held up the invoice that had been lying beside

her computer. "Do you remember this? You found it stuck to the outside of a file."

Dylan nodded, his smile fading away.

Lisa swallowed a knot of nervous tension. She had put herself in this position, after all. "There was a memo tucked inside the invoice that I didn't think much of." She pulled it out from under the invoice and handed it to Dylan. "Until I read it."

He angled her a puzzled frown as he took it. Then he read it himself.

"What in the world…?" He looked over the paper at Lisa, his eyes now a stormy gray. "Why didn't you think it was important?"

"And this invoice doesn't show up anywhere," Lisa continued, forced by her own misconduct to avoid answering his question. Deflect and distract. "I have been checking and double-checking, but it hasn't been entered in any place I can find."

Dylan didn't reply right away, as if still waiting for an answer. Then he took the invoice from her and glanced at it.

"This is for Dara's father's company." He laid it down again. "We didn't get those files."

"Why not? Dara told us she gave us everything that had been handled in the past year." Lisa finally dared to meet his gaze. "This invoice is only three months old. Two months before the accountant was fired." Lisa could not say his name, afraid that even mentioning Gabe would shout out her guilt.

Dylan took another look at the invoice, then at the memo.

"Do you think these two are connected?"

"I didn't give the invoice much consideration until this morning." Until the idea that you might be quitting made me desperate to do something. Anything. Including directing your annoyance toward me. "I think it's pertinent."

Lisa kept her eyes on the computer screen in front of her and hit a key to deactivate the screen saver. And waited.

Dylan tapped his fingers against his thigh as if trying to make up his mind. "Part of me wants to laugh off what you're saying. I want to be finished with all of this." He angled her a puzzled glance. "Yet this memo and this invoice make me think twice, even with Dara finding the money." He slapped his hands against his legs as if making up his mind. "We'll go to the office today and see if we can get into Gabe's computer. Then we can look for ourselves."

The tension in Lisa's shoulders ebbed. She had bought Gabe a little more time and another opportunity.

At what cost?

"I'll just run upstairs and change. I'll meet you at the car." She needed the paper with Gabe's password on it. She doubted Dara would give it to her. And if she had a chance, she had to risk one more call to Gabe.

Before Dylan could say anything Lisa turned and left.

Once in her room, Lisa pulled out the pants she had been wearing when she had visited Gabe last and shoved her hands into each of the pockets. Nothing.

Dylan is waiting. Hurry.

She opened her purse and riffled through it. Still nothing.

With trembling hands she grabbed her cell phone and punched Gabe's number in. No answer. Relax, relax, she told herself, and tried again. Still no answer.

She glanced around her room agitation building. Where could she have put it? She tried the pants again, then the shirt she had been wearing. As she threw it on the bed in disgust, a piece of paper fluttered to the carpet. Lisa pounced on it.

Thank You, Lord, she breathed, aware of the irony of her prayer as she glanced at Gabe's password.

I hope this works, she thought, remembering to change her clothes. She ran a quick brush through her hair and left it hanging to her shoulders. A quick glance in the mirror of the bathroom revealed pallid features dominated by wide oval eyes. *Help me through this, Lord, and I'll tell Dylan the truth. I will.*

On her way downstairs she ducked into the office, grabbed an empty computer disk and slipped it into her purse, just in case she needed a copy of whatever she might find. Continuing out the door, she went to the car where Dylan was waiting.

As they left, her heart fluttered in her chest with a mixture of nerves and anticipation. She hoped what they discovered would prove Gabe's innocence and not his guilt. And that Dara hadn't changed Gabe's password.

Chapter Eleven

Dylan turned off the street and slowed the car over the speed bump straddling the entrance to Matheson Telecom's parking lot. He glanced sidelong at Lisa, who hadn't said anything during the entire trip over. A few times he'd thought of asking her about the memo.

He didn't want to know what she had to say. He preferred to think of the time they had spent in the study that morning. Holding her in his arms. Kissing her. And most important, reading the Bible with her.

Those things were real. And those things were part of Lisa, as well. He had to believe that. His questions about the memo could come later. Once they were in Toronto they would be away from all this. And they would have a chance to pursue their changing relationship.

Where it would lead, Dylan wasn't sure. But he

knew that for now they shared a common faith, and that was the best place to begin any relationship.

He swung the car into an empty space beside his father's parking stall. Alex's silver car gleamed as it always did. His father had always taken good care of the things he owned. Stewardship, he called it. Dylan wished Alex had spent the same time and care on his company the past few years as he had on his material possessions.

He couldn't help but wonder about his mother's advice. Was confronting his dad about Ted's appointment the way to solve the current dilemma?

And even more so, did he want to be in charge?

One thing at a time.

"So, you ready to go?" he asked Lisa as he shut off the engine.

She nodded, and as soon as he had his own door open, she was out of the car.

As he followed her into the office he wondered again at her intensity, her desire to get to the bottom of this whole matter. She was the only one who seemed to really care. Other than Dara.

They didn't even bother stopping at the receptionist. Instead they went straight to Dara's office.

She sat at her desk, ramrod straight in front of her computer. Her gray suit was crisp—not a wrinkle in sight. The white shirt peeking out from the vee of her suit coat was immaculate. She wore her hair down today, softening the sharp lines of her face, but her overall appearance was one of a woman in charge, giving her the same air of control he knew all too well from the brief time he had dated her.

Except lately he had seen a few fissures in her iron restraint.

Dylan knocked lightly on her open door to announce himself.

Dara looked up, and her eyes grew wide. "What are you doing here?" Her frown deepened. "And what is *she* doing here?" Dara angled her chin toward Lisa, not even bothering to use her name.

"Last I checked, my name is still on the Matheson Telecom letterhead," Dylan said lightly, surprised at her anger. "And Lisa is helping me with this little problem."

"But we don't need any help…" Dara sputtered. "It's over. I found the money. That's why I phoned you." She pushed herself away from her desk with an abrupt movement

"I guess I wouldn't mind seeing for myself," Dylan said easily, forcing himself to stay calm as Dara stormed around the desk.

"Everything…is…fine," she said, leaning toward him, enunciating each word with harsh emphasis.

"Then it won't matter if we go looking, will it?" Dylan asked. "Just to double-check. I hauled myself all the way here from Toronto at my father's request, no less. I don't think it would be so bad if I checked things out myself." He gave her a casual smile, but his interior radar was on full alert. He'd been going through the motions to appease his father. But Dara's behavior struck a warning chord he couldn't ignore.

Why the anger? Why was she so upset? If things were truly over, as she so emphatically stated, why should she care if he checked for himself?

He thought again of the memo. Wondered at her involvement in what had happened.

Dara's eyes flicked over Lisa, then narrowed. "And you need to take her along?"

"Lisa has been gracious enough to help me. In fact, she was the one who encouraged me to finish what I started."

"And why should she care?"

Dara's question fed Dylan's niggling suspicions.

"She probably cares because she's spent quite a few days helping me. She has a time investment to consider, as well."

"But she's been compensated for that." She gave Lisa a sly glance. "Quite adequately, I'm sure."

Dylan bristled at the unpleasant insinuation threaded through her comments.

"Dylan is a generous boss," Lisa cut in, her tone full of innocence. "As I'm sure you know for yourself."

Dylan suppressed a smile. Lisa could hold her own. He caught her eye and winked. Pleasure spiraled within him when she returned his smile.

Without another word Dara turned to her desk and pulled a key out of one of the drawers. "Here's what you'll need to get into his office. It's two doors down." She scribbled a notation on a pad of paper and handed it to Dylan, but her eyes were on Lisa. "And here's his password. No promises it works. I just lucked out when I figured it out, so I may have written it wrong. I was going to get a tech in tomorrow to clean the files off it—that's why I went through it once more to see if I could find anything else. Just drop the key off here when you're done.''

''Thanks, Dara,'' Dylan said, taking the paper and handing it directly to Lisa. ''You've been most co-operative.''

She didn't say anything—just kept staring at Lisa. ''You live in Toronto?'' she asked all of a sudden.

Lisa gave a start, but nodded.

''East York?''

''Why do you ask?''

''Just curious'' was her cryptic comment. She turned to Dylan. ''Happy hunting,'' she said with a faint smile. ''Just close the door on your way out.''

Gabe's office had been emptied of everything but a desk and his computer, but it still held a faint musty smell of papers.

''We may as well get started,'' Dylan said, fidgeting while Lisa booted up the computer. He thought of the promise he had made his brother, then wondered why Ted was so anxious to have him back off.

''We'll start with that bank account,'' he said, pacing around the desk. ''Try to see if you can find it somewhere.''

He stopped behind her, then started pacing again.

''Dylan,'' Lisa said, glancing up at him, ''why don't you get a coffee or something?''

Dylan held her gaze. Smiled at her. ''You trying to get rid of me?''

''Your prowling is making me nervous.''

''Do you want anything?''

She shook her head, looking back at the computer. She glanced at the paper Dara had given them and punched in the combination of letters and numbers, frowning in concentration.

"Okay. I'll leave you to it. Be back in a bit." He paused, waiting for some kind of sign that things were still the same between them, but she wasn't looking at him. As he walked down the hall to the coffee room he wondered again at her desire to get to the bottom of this.

Relief swept through Lisa when Dylan finally closed the door behind him. Now she could work in private.

Dara's password hadn't gotten her in. That was no surprise to Lisa.

She carefully slipped Gabe's password out of her pocket, then punched it in. The pattern seemed vaguely familiar, but she didn't have time to puzzle it out. She hit Enter.

And she was in. She put the paper back into her pocket.

She thought she'd start with the easy stuff. On a hunch she clicked the icon showing her the most recently used documents. And there they were. One labeled Wilson Engineering, Dara's father's company. The other was a number that she suspected was the company account.

Lisa highlighted the files she thought she needed, and while she copied them to the disk drive she flicked through the properties. From what she could see the files had been accessed just this morning. And the numbered account looked as if it had been created after Gabe left.

Exhilaration pumped through her. This information, combined with the memo, could be just what she needed to clear Gabe's name.

Seconds later the disk in the drive was whirring, saving the information she had found. She pulled the diskette out of the drive and slipped it into her purse just as she heard a light knock on the door.

She quickly restarted the computer. Thankfully the speakers weren't connected, so no little ditty gave her actions away.

"How's it coming?" Dara swept into the office and came to stand beside Lisa.

"I'm having some problems logging on," Lisa said, making a show of glancing at the paper Dara had given her. "I've tried this one a couple of times."

"I may have written it down wrong." Dara took the paper from Lisa, but she didn't look at it. Instead she looked at Lisa more closely. "You know, I've said this before, but you look very familiar."

Lisa shrugged the comment off, uncomfortable under Dara's relentless scrutiny. "I'm fairly unremarkable."

"That's not very complimentary to yourself, is it?"

"I know who I am."

"Do you? I wish I did. Know who you are."

Fear tingled up her neck, but Lisa held Dara's gaze, projecting innocence. "Why? I'm only around for a short while. Soon Dylan and I will be going back to Toronto."

"Yes. And Dylan will be leaving Matheson Telecom.'' Dara's smile held no warmth. ''And it would only be fair if I added, 'and leaving you.' Dylan is like that, you see. Has never held on to a girl for longer than a few weeks.'' Dara scribbled something on the paper. ''Try this one.''

Lisa glanced at it and forced a polite smile. Another useless password. ''Thanks for this.'' She looked back up at Dara. ''And the advice.''

Dara waved a careless hand at her. ''Think nothing of it.''

I'll try not to think of you at all. Lisa waited until Dara closed the door behind her, then folded up the piece of paper and slipped it into her pocket. She wasn't going to waste any more time playing Dara's games. She hoped she had what she had come for.

She turned Gabe's computer off, looking around his office.

What hopes had he brought to this job? she wondered, trailing her hand over his desk. He had been so excited when he phoned her to tell her about the job. All the hard work and sacrifices she had made had been worth every moment.

She slipped her purse over her shoulder and got up. Once she showed Dylan what she suspected, Gabe's name would be cleared.

And hers would be mud.

She thought of the wondrous moments with Dylan in the study. When he had read the Bible to her.

Love is patient. Love is kind.

Would he be patient with what she had to say when she finally dared tell him the truth? That afternoon on the sailboat he had spoken so strongly of how important trust was to him. How it had hurt when his father had broken trust with him.

Could he forgive her for what she had done to him? Would he understand?

She pressed her fingers to her aching forehead, praying, unsure what to ask for. What to say. Now that she had proof that her brother was innocent, she felt curiously deflated. She wanted to help her brother, but the cost had been too high.

Why had Dylan come into her life this way? Why couldn't they have simply met under normal circumstances? A man and a woman who were attracted to each other.

But it hadn't happened that way. She had sought him out. Had used him and his family.

How could she face them?

She drew in a deep breath. She had made her own decisions. She had made her own mistakes. She knew what God required of her and what she had to do. When she and Dylan got home she was going to show him what she had discovered. And then she was going to tell him the truth.

She strode out of the office, looking for Dylan. One more step and this would all be over.

There was no fresh coffee made in the coffee room. Dylan pulled a face at the dark brew sitting in the glass pot.

He should go back to Lisa, but was strangely reluctant to do so. He would have thought the moment they had shared in the study would have brought them closer together. And it had.

For a while.

And then she had retreated.

And he had read the memo that she had lied to him about.

The thought stuck in his mind, like a dirty stick that wouldn't be dislodged. Why hadn't she shown him right away? He didn't quite believe her excuse that she'd thought it unimportant. Lisa was thorough and diligent.

Restless again, he walked over to his father's office. His secretary was gone, but the door to Alex's office was open. To Dylan's surprise, his father was inside. Dylan knocked lightly on the door.

Alex stood by the window, his arms crossed. His suit coat hung crookedly on the back of his chair, and his tie was undone. Dylan was taken aback. At the office, his father always presented nothing less than a professional appearance.

Alex glanced back over his shoulder, and when he saw Dylan he gave him a tired smile. "This is a surprise, Dylan. What brings you here?"

"Dara phoned this morning," Dylan said. "She said she found the missing money in a bank account set up by Gabe."

"I heard that." Alex rubbed the back of his neck with a slow movement as if even that was too much effort for him, staring out the window again. "Is that why you came?"

Dylan carefully closed the door behind them, but didn't bother to sit down himself. He was here now. Might as well get straight to the point.

"The night of your anniversary Ted had a talk

with me, Dad. He asked me to back off this investigation. Why would he do that?''

Alex slowly turned to face him, sorrow lining his face. ''Ted and Dara have been under a lot of pressure the past few weeks. Actually the past few months. This whole business with the accountant has made things even more difficult for them. Ted feels threatened by your presence here, Dylan.''

''Why should he, Dad? From what I understand he doesn't even want to be in charge of the company.''

''I know.''

Dylan thought of the conversation he'd had with his mother just that morning. Could she be right? Was his father waiting for some kind of direction? Some kind of leadership?

''At the risk of bringing up old history, it makes me wonder again why you gave him the job you promised me.''

Alex sighed and dropped into his chair. ''Please sit down, Dylan.''

''I can't stay too long, Dad. Lisa is with me. She's busy in Gabe's office right now.''

''Doing what?''

''Trying to find out whatever we can from his computer.''

''Well, I won't keep you, then.''

And for the first time since he had come home, Dylan got a sense of what his mother was saying. Alex looked beaten. Tired.

''I've got to go.'' But he stayed where he was, suddenly reluctant to leave. In two days he would be back in Toronto, and then in a few weeks finally free from Matheson Telecom.

What would happen to the company then? Ted didn't want the responsibilities he had, nor was he capable of carrying them out. His father looked as if he was carrying too much himself. He looked broken and weary.

Dylan thought of pride. His own. His father's. And he knew what he had to do.

"We'll talk again, Dad," he said softly. "I promise."

"I'd like that," Alex said, a faint smile pulling on his mouth.

And as Dylan walked back to Gabe's office he felt as if events were slowly falling more heavily on his shoulders, pushing him in different directions. He had thought he had his life all mapped out before he came here. The company he would be working for was up-and-coming. Not direct competition to Matheson Telecom, but it had the potential to be. He would be in on the ground floor—a fancy term for starting over.

And he would be working the same crazy long hours he had when he first started the Toronto branch, trying to prove to his father and himself that he was worthy.

Was it worth it?

A few days ago he had gone sailing with a woman who was slowly becoming special to him. He was actually building a relationship with someone he cared for.

Because he had taken the time for it.

What would happen to him and Lisa when he left Matheson Telecom? When he immersed himself in a new job? A new place where he had to prove himself all over again.

"Hey, Dylan."

Dylan spun around as Lisa walked out of his thoughts and into his line of sight. She was smiling. "I got what we came for. I want to have another look at it on the computer at home."

Dylan looked down at her, his own questions about her spinning around his mind, melding with the ones about his father.

He didn't want to go to the computer at home. He didn't want to think about crooked accountants. Fathers who made mistakes.

Decisions he had to make.

He wanted them to be together as they had been on the boat. As they had been for that magical moment in the gazebo. When all he had to worry about was how often he thought he could get away with kissing her.

Lord, I don't know what to do. I'm too confused. Too mixed up about my father. My brother.

Lisa.

"Are you okay?" Lisa caught him by the arm and gave it a light shake.

Cast all your anxieties on him.

He certainly had enough to cast.

"Let's go home," he said, covering her hand with his.

She nodded and they left.

"Were you able to find anything?" Dylan asked

as they got into the car. "You weren't in there very long."

"I only needed to copy the most recently used files, and I found those right away."

"You didn't want to look at them while you were there anyway?"

"Some of the programs I would need for that were taken off the computer."

"I'll be mighty glad when this is all over," he said, starting the car and pulling out of the parking lot. "I sure hope whatever you've got on that disk will finish this once and for all."

"I was so sure I copied the files properly," Lisa said, staring at the error message on her computer screen, her heart filling her throat. How could this have happened?

She hit a key, shut down the program and started over again, trying to keep the panic at bay.

Dylan stood beside her, his arms crossed. "Do you remember the names of the files? I could get Dara to e-mail them to us as an attachment."

"No. I don't think that would work." The last thing she wanted was for Dara to know that she had gotten into Gabe's computer. Especially when Dara had given them the wrong password in the first place. "I think part of the problem is the programs. I might not have the right one on this computer to open it." She opened up another window, trying to search for a program that might be able to read the file. Still nothing.

Dylan rocked lightly, then picked up the memo

again. "You know what would make the most sense?" he said softly.

"What?" Lisa asked, turning to him.

He looked down at her, his mouth lifted in a smile.

Lisa felt the too-familiar push and pull of her longing for him and the reality of their situation.

"If my father would hire an auditor and stop trying to solve this thing internally." Dylan crouched beside her. "But that won't happen."

Lisa looked down at Dylan, resisting the urge to touch him. Her affection for him grew stronger every day. And alongside her changing feelings for him had come a renewal in her faith life. This morning he had read to her from the Bible, and for a brief and shining moment all was well in her world. She had felt close to him. Close to the Lord. The peace she had been seeking for so long, the love she had been waiting for was all there, surrounding her and holding her up.

But she knew that in the next day or so she had to choose. Obedience, or a relationship that had started with a lie.

"So, we can't pursue that," Dylan said, pushing himself up. "Let's get out of here. I've spent too much time here already."

He reached out to Lisa. She glanced once more at the blank computer screen, hope dying within her.

Tonight she had to find a way to contact Gabe and tell him that she had done all she could for him.

But for now she took Dylan's hand and let him pull her up into his arms. She allowed herself a moment to enjoy the warmth and strength of his embrace before she pulled away.

Dylan pulled Lisa a bit closer, brushing the top of her head with his chin. "You're awfully quiet tonight," he said.

"Most people don't like to chat when they're watching a movie," Lisa murmured, pulling away from him and drawing her sweater around her.

Dylan picked up the remote as the credits of the movie started rolling and turned the television off. "Well, the movie is done—you can chat now."

"Hard to do on demand." Lisa curled on her side of the couch, looking everywhere but at him.

During the movie she had been more than content to cuddle up against him. Now that it was over, she had withdrawn as she had this afternoon when they had come back from the office.

He wished they could go back to this morning. That precious moment of connection he had felt with her. Short of pulling out the Bible again, he wasn't quite sure how to re-create that.

Love is patient.

He knew what he had to do. Let go. Let God. Put everything in His hands. Even Lisa.

"Once we're back in Toronto, Lisa, nothing has to change between us. Just because you won't be my secretary anymore doesn't mean…" He let the awkward sentence lie heavily between them.

Very suave, he thought, repressing a frown. What was it about her that turned him inside out?

Lisa moved closer, pulling one of his hands into

hers. She pressed it to her cheek, and hope bloomed in Dylan.

"I don't deserve this, you know," she said softly, still avoiding his gaze. "You are the most wonderful person I've ever met. This morning…" She paused, her voice catching on the words. She drew in a deep breath and continued. "This morning I felt closer to God than I have since my parents died. This morning I felt a touch of the peace that I knew God could give me." She looked up at him now. Dylan was shocked to see her eyes brimming with tears. "I want to thank you for that. And for so much more." She leaned closer to him and touched her lips to his cheek. "You are an amazing person, Dylan Matheson." And as she drew away, three faintly whispered words tantalized him.

I love you.

But before he could ask her if he'd heard right, she was off the couch and running down the hallway to the stairs.

Chapter Twelve

''Lisa, please open the door. We need to talk.''

Lisa hunched down on the floor, holding her arms over her head, praying Dylan would leave. She couldn't talk to him now.

Dylan tried the door, the rattle of the doorknob sending a chill down Lisa's back. He gave another knock, then stormed off.

Forgive me, Lord, she prayed. Forgive me, Dylan.

She waited a few more moments, then opened up her cell phone, its outline wavering in her vision. Tears slipped from her eyes as she punched in Gabe's number. As she clutched the phone to her ear she heard Dylan's car spinning down the driveway, the sound an angry counterpoint to the shrill ringing of Gabe's phone.

What had she done?

She had agreed to watch the movie with Dylan only because the girls were going to join them. Then one of the twins' friends called. Something better was going on somewhere else, and Amber and Erika were gone. Mr. and Mrs. Matheson had gone out for supper with some friends.

So it was just Dylan and Lisa alone in the house, which had proved to be too intimate. Too dangerous.

She hadn't meant to tell him she loved him. The words had come out, pushed past the walls she'd been slowly trying to rebuild against him.

Lisa palmed her tears away, sniffing as she willed Gabe to answer. She had to talk to him. Had to connect and remind herself of her main purpose.

"Hello?"

"Gabe, it's me. Lisa."

"I'm so glad you called. Did you find anything? What's the matter? Are you okay?"

"No. Well…yes." She sniffed.

Her phone beeped in her ear and Gabe's voice cut off.

"Gabe. Are you there?" Lisa pressed the phone closer.

Nothing. She glanced at the screen. Her battery was dead.

Lisa threw the phone down and pressed the heels of her hands against her eyes as if holding back the confusion of her thoughts. Now what? She needed to talk to Gabe. Tell him what was happening, then confess everything to Dylan.

Gabe. Dylan. Both bounced back and forth, each creating a mixture of emotions.

She loved Dylan.

She had lied to Dylan.

Gabe was innocent.

Lisa jumped off the bed and grabbed her coat. She had to talk to Gabe. This back and forth was wearing her down, confusing her more than anything she'd had to deal with before.

It wasn't right to keep deceiving Dylan and it was wrong to go against what she knew God wanted for her. But before she told Dylan what was happening, she had to tell Gabe what she was planning.

She slipped downstairs and quickly called a cab, praying one would come before anyone came home. As she opened the door, the shrill ring of the phone echoed through the empty house. Lisa's heart leaped into her throat.

She didn't dare answer and quickly stepped outside. The cool evening drizzle dampened her hair and she shivered into her coat. She didn't want to wait in the house.

Then twin cones of light swept up the drive and Lisa ducked back into the tall shrubs lining the driveway. As the vehicle turned around, relief made her legs weak. It was her cab.

She slipped into the vehicle and gave the driver directions to Gabe's place. Then she sat back and prayed as the cab drove down the hill, blending into the traffic heading across the inlet.

Vancouver was hard enough to navigate in the dark and the rain. Trying to follow a vehicle made it even harder.

Thankfully the light on top of the cab made it easier to spot.

Dylan knew he'd never make a spy or detective. After almost losing the cab on Lions Gate Bridge, he opted for staying fairly close, hoping neither the driver nor Lisa would notice him following.

He felt heartsick and ashamed, but Dara's phone call to his cell phone just before he came home from his aimless drive had fed his own confusion. And when he saw the cab pull out of his parents' driveway just as he was returning, he knew he had to follow.

The cab finally pulled up in front of a dingy apartment building, and as Dylan drove slowly past the vehicle, he saw Lisa get out, pay the driver and walk over to the doorway. He kept going, pulled in to the nearest alley and turned off his car.

Now what? Follow her again? Try to talk to her again?

He locked up his car feeling more and more foolish, and strode down the wet sidewalk. What if this was all just an innocent mistake? What if the person Lisa was seeing was just an old friend? Maybe even a boyfriend.

I love you.

He was sure he hadn't imagined that. So why had she run away? Again?

Dylan stopped in front of the doorway Lisa had gone through and looked at the names beside the numbers. Most of them were faded, but one had a fresh name printed beside it. Haskell.

Dylan's heart dropped like a stone. Dara was right.

"I can prove that Dara put the money into that account, Gabe. I saw on the computer that the money was transferred after you left."

Gabe leaned back in his chair smiling a tired smile. "If you can't read the disk, you don't have proof."

"I was hoping you could have a look at it."

"On what?" Gabe waved his hand around the sparse furnishings of the apartment.

Lisa chewed her lower lip, trying to think. "Is there some kind of Internet café around here? They'd have computers."

"That's not going to work. I left Matheson Telecom in the morning. If it was set up after I left, and you can get on my computer to prove it, then you might have proof."

"I doubt I could get in again. If Dara knows I got in, all she would have to do is change the password."

"Or corrupt the files. I'm surprised she didn't do that anyway. And you said she's getting a tech in to clean off the computer tomorrow." Gabe sighed, leaning back in his chair. "May as well give up, Lisa. Things just aren't working our way."

Lisa sank into the chair across from Gabe. "So what do we do?"

"I guess I just take that other job."

Lisa shook her head and held her hands up. "No. Gabe. Don't do that."

Gabe banged his hand against the table, his sudden anger startling Lisa. "You're so full of advice on what I should and shouldn't do." He ground out the words. "You haven't done a thing for me. Nothing."

His words shot straight to her heart, plunging in like a knife. "How dare you say that, Gabe?" she asked, squeezing her hands together as if holding back her hurt. "Everything I've ever done has been for you," she said softly. "Getting the job. Coming out here. Pretending to be Dylan's girlfriend." Her voice caught on Dylan's name.

Silence dropped between them, broken only by the muffled sounds of traffic outside. Feet walking down the hall inside.

Lisa drew in a long slow breath, willing her own erratic emotions to soften. "I've put a lot on the line for you, Gabe. More than you can know."

She felt Gabe's hands on her shoulders and she reached up to cover one with her own.

"I'm sorry, Lisa. You're right," Gabe said.

A light knock at the door was her only warning.

"It's open," Gabe called.

And Dylan walked in.

Lisa dropped her hand and pulled away from Gabe, shock sending ice through her veins. Too late. Too late.

The words echoed mockingly through her head as she stood to face Dylan, her red cheeks condemning her more than anything she could say.

Dylan's eyes flicked from Lisa to Gabe and back again, the dim light of the apartment casting harsh shadows across his face.

"How long has this been going on?" His voice whipped through the air.

Lisa wet her lips, trying to find the right words, the right way to explain her subterfuge. "I'm sorry, Dylan. I should have told you."

He took a step back, as if trying to keep as much

distance between them as possible. "Didn't your *boyfriend* mind all the time we spent together?"

"No. You've got this all wrong." Lisa held out her hand to him, entreating him, realizing how the scene Dylan had stumbled on must have looked to him.

"Lisa is my stepsister. She came here to help me," Gabe said, anger edging his voice.

Dylan's sharp laugh stripped away most of the hope Lisa still held on to. "Why don't I feel relieved about that?"

Lisa could say nothing in her defense. Nothing that would change the bitter reality of what he was saying. She felt Gabe's hand on her shoulder. A small comfort.

"Is this why you took the job?"

"I wanted to help my brother. Yes."

"Were you ever going to tell me?"

Lisa fought down the panic that threatened to choke her. She could feel her future crumbling beneath her feet, but even as she struggled to salvage the tiniest step, the anger and betrayal in Dylan's eyes showed her it was doomed. She said nothing.

"I'll bring your things tomorrow on my way to the airport."

The icy finality in his voice cooled any shred of hope she had clung to.

"If it's okay with you, I would like to come to the house to pick them up. I'll come after you leave."

"I don't want you to bother my family."

"She just wants to get her stuff, Dylan…" Gabe began.

Though thankful for his defense, Lisa shook her head. "I want to tell your parents and family myself what I did," she said to Dylan. "I believe I need to confess to them."

Dylan caught her pleading glance. Hesitated.

"Why did you lie to me, Lisa?"

He was still talking. A flicker of hope. "I had to do it to get the job. To get close to your father," she said, the truth sounding even more stark spoken aloud.

"All necessary for your role."

Lisa couldn't reply; her actions condemned her as much as Dylan's words did.

"So everything that happened, all the things we shared were fake? Just part of this role you were playing?"

"Those were real, Dylan," Lisa cried, her heart breaking at the angry hurt in his voice. "I meant everything I ever said to you."

Dylan lowered his hand, his eyes now cold. Sharp. "All the secret phone calls, the mysterious trips were about helping out someone who stole from the company—the company I'm a part of?"

"I didn't steal anything," Gabe snapped. "And if Lisa lied to you, it was because of me. I'm the one you should be angry with. Not her."

"I wanted to help Gabe," Lisa said, wishing he could understand at least a small part of her reasons.

Dylan's gaze stayed on Lisa, his anger directed solely toward her. "You know, I really thought we had something," he said. "For the first time..." He stopped there.

"I think we did, Dylan." Lisa fought down her panic at the words they were using. *Had. Did.* Past tense. "I care for you. And I was going to tell you about Gabe. But I had to take care of my brother first."

"Why?"

Lisa drew some small sliver of hope from even that one word. From the little she knew about Dylan, he didn't stay to talk when he was angry. He left.

"Gabe is all I have in the world. Everything I've ever done has been for him. So when I found out he was fired, I knew it couldn't be true. And I had to help him." She willed the right words to come. Prayed for the right thing to say. "Family takes care of family. We help and take care of each other. And make sacrifices." Lisa took a small step closer to Dylan, holding his eyes, praying he would understand, even though she knew she didn't deserve even that. "I've struggled more than you can know about what to do. I've prayed about this…."

"Prayed? Pardon me while I try to work my head around this. You prayed about how you were going to lie to all of us?"

Lisa pressed her hands to her chest, struggling to find the right words. *Please help me, Lord. I know I was wrong, but I'm trying to make this right.*

"When I first started working for you, my faith didn't mean much. So it was easy to deceive you. But going to church with your family, watching them and listening to them brought me back to the faith I used to have. I knew I was wrong, but didn't know when to tell you." She felt Gabe come up beside her and lay his hand on her shoulder as if to give her strength. She looked up, holding Dylan's angry gaze. "I found something precious with your family, Dylan. Their faith is an example to me. But more important, I found something precious with you. When we read the Bible together, for the first time in my life I felt something pure and true and right happening in my life. I'm not perfect, Dylan. My faith is weak. But I discovered something important in the time we spent together. Something I don't want to let go of."

"That seems convenient, Lisa."

Hurt, she pulled back, closer to Gabe. Her brother. "You know it's true, Dylan."

"What do you know about truth? You're no different than Dara. Actually you're better. At lying. You certainly had me fooled."

He spun around and left, the click of the apartment door sounding like a gunshot in the silence.

Dylan rested his hands on the steering wheel of the car, staring at his parents' house, rain pattering on the roof of the car. His anger had had a chance to cool, but his frustration and mistrust still simmered below the surface.

I trusted her, Lord. I believed in her.

As he trudged up the walk, rain slipping down his neck, he wondered what his next step should be.

Give it all up?

And leave Lisa behind when he left for Toronto tomorrow?

The thought spun through his mind, bringing sorrow and hurt in its wake. But what else was he going to do?

He shook his coat off and hung it in one of the massive cupboards just off the foyer. The house was eerily silent. A thin sliver of light slipped out from under the door of the study and Dylan walked toward it. He didn't want to be alone.

His father sat in one of the chairs, the light beside him creating an intimate atmosphere.

As Dylan came in, Alex looked up from the book he was reading. "I thought you and Lisa had decided to stay home."

Dylan sank onto a couch and massaged the back of his neck. "We did. Then we had a disagreement."

"Do you want to talk about it?"

"I don't know what to say." He laughed shortly. "I don't know what to think."

Alex thankfully didn't acknowledge the vague comment but put his book down, his attention focused completely on his son. "Do you want to tell me what is wrong, Dylan?"

Dylan blew his breath out and looked over at his father. Saw again the lines that bracketed his mouth. The weariness he'd noticed this afternoon. The same weariness he felt himself.

"I just found out that Lisa is Gabe Haskell's sister." As he spoke the words aloud Dylan felt again the twist of betrayal.

"How do you know that?"

"Dara phoned me this evening. Told me that she suspected there was a connection between Lisa and Gabe. So I followed Lisa this evening and found her at Gabe Haskell's apartment.'' Dylan pushed himself off the couch. He paced around the room, his agitation and frustration needing an outlet. "She never told me who she was when she applied for the job. Never said anything about her brother. And all she could say now was that family takes care of family. Like it's some kind of creed she lives by."

"It's not a bad one."

"And that takes precedence over truth and what is right?'' Dylan stopped behind a chair, grasping the back of it with his hands. "He stole from us, Dad. He took money that didn't belong to him. And his sister spent time with us as a family pretending to be someone she wasn't. She didn't just lie to me. She lied to all of you. So don't stand up for her."

"I'm not so sure Gabe stole from us."

His softly spoken words caught Dylan's full attention. "What?"

"I never truly believed he did. And if he did, he didn't do it alone."

Don't know if I can keep doing this. Ted needs to know.

The words of the memo sifted back into his memory. The memo that Lisa had hidden from him. The memo that had been attached to an invoice they couldn't trace.

Dylan pulled his hands over his face, wishing he had a few moments to think. To figure out what was really going on. "Can you please explain what you're talking about?'' he asked tiredly.

"Sit down, Dylan. We need to have that talk we were supposed to have this afternoon. And you're leaving tomorrow. So now is the only time we have.''

Dylan lowered himself onto the couch again and laid his head back. ''First tell me—if you think Gabe didn't do it, why did you ask me to come here?''

Alex leaned forward, his hands clasped. ''I wasn't sure enough about Gabe's guilt or innocence. But I couldn't allow him to stay with the company as long as there was any shadow hanging over his name.'' Alex sighed lightly. ''I had suspected for a while that if Gabe had done it, Dara was involved. And if Dara was involved, I suspected Ted was, as well.''

''What do you mean?'' Dylan frowned, trying to grasp this new information. ''How did you come to that conclusion?''

''I didn't allow Ted complete free rein over the company when I let him take over.'' Alex tilted Dylan a wry smile. ''In spite of what you think, I wasn't entirely sure of Ted's abilities, either.''

''Which makes me wonder again and again why you put him in charge.''

''I know that's a sore point with you, Dylan. And I know I did wrong by you.'' Alex got up slowly. Walked over to the window and stared out, as if trying to find answers there. ''Like I told you this afternoon, I am well aware of Ted's failings. I am also well aware of your abilities. I guess I was hoping, in some foolish way, that the older brother would take on some of the characteristics of his younger brother given the right circumstances.''

''You told me it was because he was married.''

"That was a very important reason. Ted had extra responsibilities when he and Dara married."

"Married very quickly, I might add," Dylan said.

Alex turned to Dylan. "I doubt Dara ever told you why she broke up with you and married Ted so quickly?"

Dylan shook his head. What he had just lost seemed infinitely more precious than the shallow relationship he and Dara had had those many years ago. It no longer mattered.

"Dara told us she was expecting Ted's child. Her father insisted they get married. Ted felt the same way. He loved Dara. So they got married." Alex opened his hands in a gesture of surrender. "I could have given Ted the Toronto job instead of you, but I wanted him closer to home where we could give them some guidance and direction."

Dylan stared at his father as his words swirled around, a chaos of ideas and sounds. "But they don't have..." His voice trailed off.

"It turned out that Dara wasn't pregnant after all," Alex said softly.

Dylan lost his breath as the conversation shifted into unknown territory. Anger followed close behind.

"Why didn't anyone tell me?" he cried, hurt pushing the words out as he faced down his father. "Ted is my brother. I care what happens to him."

Alex smiled a gentle smile. "I'm sorry, Dylan. We wanted to tell you, but Ted was adamant that we keep it quiet. Especially from you."

"Why?" Dylan could only stare at his father, trying to comprehend what his brother had gone through.

"Because of your history with Dara. And, I suspect, because he thought that Dara had come to him on the rebound from you."

"But I'm his brother. This is my family. Surely I had a right to know."

"In hindsight, yes, we should have told you. I wanted to a number of times, but I think Ted felt a mixture of guilt and shame over what had happened."

Dylan's perceptions shifted as he tried to keep up. All his previous knowledge of his brother took on a different hue. One idea pushed to the surface, startling in its clarity.

They weren't so different after all.

Ted had been duped by his girlfriend, too.

"I wish I had known." Dylan pulled his hands over his face. "I would have been here for him." He closed his eyes as he thought of Ted, caught in events that pulled him along to places he didn't want to go. Thought of himself and Lisa.

"We thought that Dara and Ted loved each other. But I'm worried about their relationship now."

"Was Dara involved with the accountant? With Gabe?"

"I don't think so."

"I keep coming back to the question—why did you want me to come? Why didn't you hire an outside auditor?"

"Because Ted had gone through enough with Dara. I was hoping that if you came, if Dara knew that you would be looking around, she would cave in and let me know what was really going on. And if Ted was involved, I wanted to find out from him.''

''I don't think he was, or is. Lisa showed me a memo that Gabe had written to Dara. In it he said he didn't know if he could keep doing this and that Ted needed to know. To me it implicates Gabe and, at the same time, Dara.''

''Do you have a copy of this memo?''

Dylan nodded, feeling again the sting of humiliation when he thought of Lisa and what she had done to him.

''I want to show it to Dara. To see what she will say.''

''I think you've given Dara enough chances, Dad. I think it's time you do what I've been asking you to do for a while now. Bring in an outside auditor.''

''I will, but not right away. I am still hoping that if Dara knows what we know, she'll come clean. It would save your brother further humiliation.''

Dylan acknowledged this small concession with a curt nod. His father's defense of Ted made more sense, but he still didn't like it.

''I sense you're not happy with that.'' Alex sat on the coffee table across from Dylan, leaning toward him, his elbows resting on his knees. ''I'm not, either. But it would be freeing for Dara to have a chance to confess. To realize that in spite of what we know we are still giving her a chance. God gives us many, many chances, too, Dylan. I think it would be unwise and uncaring of me not to do the same for Dara.''

Dylan remembered his mother's comment about secrets. "Does Mom know about all this?"

"She knows about Ted and Dara, of course. But I haven't told her about my suspicions about Dara. I didn't want to worry her. She's had enough on her mind about them as it is."

"I think you should tell her what's happening. Sometimes the things we dream up can be worse than the reality."

Alex looked up and held Dylan's gaze. "I'm hoping the same can be said for you."

"What do you mean?"

"I have something to ask of you, Dylan. I didn't do what I promised and I know it's caused a lot of bitterness for you. My only feeble excuse is that I felt trapped and caught by my concern for Ted. It wasn't that I loved him more. It was just that I knew he needed me more. I want to ask your forgiveness for not giving you the job I promised. For not being the father to you that I should have. I don't deserve it, but I have to ask."

Dylan looked up at his father. Saw again the shadow of sorrow in his father's eyes. Thought of the burden he had been carrying all this time. Thought of the sorrow that could have been averted if only Alex had told him everything.

But would he have listened?

"I think you need to know that I love you, Dylan," Alex continued quietly. "And that I want to make things right between us. My pride has caused problems. Pride in my family. In my company. But I think God has brought me to a place where I've learned to let go of that.'' He pushed himself to his feet and walked away. ''I'm sorry, Dylan,'' he said, standing by the window again. ''Sorry for wasting your time this past week and sorry for wasting those years of your life.''

''But my years weren't wasted, Dad,'' Dylan said, the truth coming to him in a flash of insight. ''I learned to work on my own. To stop seeking your approval and to appreciate my strengths. And as for the past week...'' He stopped there.

''This past week,'' his father prompted, ''you had time to spend with your girlfriend. A girl, I must say, we have been very pleased with in spite of what you've just told me about her.''

His father's approval of Lisa was bittersweet.

And suddenly truth washed over Dylan. He wasn't innocent, either.

''I also have a confession to make, Dad,'' he said softly, cringing at his own pride. His own duplicity. ''When we first came here Lisa and I weren't really dating. Yes, she's my secretary, but I asked her to pretend to be my girlfriend. To keep Mom and the girls off my back.''

''I don't blame you,'' Alex said with a smile.

In spite of the intensity of the moment, Dylan had to laugh.

''And what is your relationship now?'' Alex asked.

Dylan sighed. ''It changed, grew. But now I don't know what to think about her anymore.''

''Do you love her?''

''I've never felt this way before.''

"Sounds to me pretty close to love."

"So what do I do?"

"Give her a chance. Like I was willing to give Dara a chance. Like God gives us a chance every minute of every day."

"But how can I carry on a relationship that was built on deceit?"

Alex laid his hand on Dylan's shoulder. "Yours or hers?"

That was it. Dylan knew he had no right to be angry with Lisa.

"Lisa has been on her own for years," Alex continued. "Gabe is her only family member. Give her credit for taking care of him in the only way she knew how. God works in mysterious ways, Dylan. Maybe everything came together for a purpose."

Chapter Thirteen

The early-morning breeze brushed over Dylan as he hunched over the Bible he had taken out on the deck. He had hardly slept all night, reliving again and again the words he had thrown at Lisa in anger.

Love is patient, love is kind. It does not envy, it does not boast, it is not proud.

Dylan read and reread the passage he and Lisa had shared just yesterday. Remembered what she had told him. Family takes care of family. As his father had taken care of Ted.

He continued. *Love does not delight in evil, but rejoices in truth.*

The reality he had to face was that he had no more right to get angry with Lisa over her deception than his family did over his.

But their relationship that had started with deception had become truth. She had become special to him. He loved her.

The words settled quietly into his mind and stayed. He loved her.

He had never been able to say that about anyone else before, but he knew for a certainty that this was real.

Dylan closed the Bible and looked out over the bay, past the office buildings. Somewhere out there was the dingy apartment block where Lisa had spent the night.

He shouldn't have walked out on her, he thought with a pang of shame. But the hurt and pride had been too great. But how could he go back?

What do I do, Lord? How can I fix this?

He thought of what his father had told him last night, heard once again the faintly whispered words Lisa had spoken last night, just before she had gone upstairs. Before she left for Gabe's. *I love you.*

Help me, Lord, to overcome my own pride. Love is not proud.

"Good morning, Dylan."

He glanced up to see Amber standing in the doorway, her hair artfully arranged in a style reminiscent of Lisa's funky hairdos.

"Hey, there. How come you're all dressed up?"

Amber frowned at him. "How come you're not? You were going to drop me off downtown on your way to the airport this morning."

His flight to Toronto. His important meeting with his future business partners. He had forgotten about both.

"What time is it?"

"Seven o'clock. I need to be downtown at eight, and your flight leaves at nine-thirty."

Panic tightened his midsection. How could he have forgotten?

But he had to talk to Lisa before he left. Try to salvage something from yesterday's mess.

If he rushed, he might be able to squeeze a few more minutes out of his schedule. It wasn't enough time to fix what had gone wrong, but he couldn't leave Vancouver without one last try.

Maybe he could convince her to at least listen.

"Can you be a bit earlier?" he asked, jumping up from his chair. "I'll meet you at the car in five."

"But Mom, Dad and Erika want to say goodbye. They're just getting up."

"Don't have time. I'll call them from the airport."

Upstairs, he threw his clothes into the suitcase, not even bothering to fold or hang up. He didn't shave— he could do that once he landed in Toronto. He threw into his carry-on what he needed for the meeting and ran downstairs.

"Get in the car," he called to Amber as he tossed his suitcase into the trunk. "Let's go."

"Where's Lisa?" Amber asked as Dylan spun out of the driveway. "Isn't she coming along? I wanted to say goodbye to her."

"She's staying at a friend's. I'll be seeing her after I drop you off." He accelerated down the hill and ran a yellow light to get onto the main avenue leading downtown. "I have something very important to talk to her about."

"What is that?" Amber twisted in her seat, grinning at her brother in expectation.

"Pride and deceit and love."

Amber pulled a face as she sank back in her seat. "That's pretty heavy, but it doesn't sound like a proposal to me."

"No, it doesn't. But it's a start," Dylan said, swerving into an opening in traffic. He ignored the sudden blaring of the truck's horn and scooted into another opening.

"You're driving like a crazy man, Dylan. What is wrong with you?"

"Nothing. Everything."

Please, Lord, just let me get to the apartment in time. Give me a chance to talk to her.

Ten minutes later he rocked to a halt in front of the Convention Centre downtown. He returned Amber's hug with a perfunctory one. "Gotta go, kiddo. You take care."

"Dylan, what is going on?"

"I'll call you—"

"From the airport," Amber interrupted. "Go, already. If you don't have time to properly say goodbye to your family, then forget it." She flounced out of the car and didn't look back.

Dylan didn't have time to feel guilty. He had more important things on his mind.

By the time he pulled up in front of Gabe's apartment, his heart was pumping. He had one hour. One hour to convince Lisa that he was wrong. To ask her to forgive him. To tell Gabe that his father had his doubts about his guilt.

He just hoped Lisa was still here. As he jogged down the sidewalk to the front door, he wondered how he was going to get in. Lisa or Gabe would hardly buzz him up when he announced himself. Thankfully, someone was leaving just as he got there and he caught the door before it closed.

Hurry. Hurry. He charged up the stairs two at a time and skidded to a halt in front of Gabe's apartment.

He took a moment to catch his breath. To send up a quick prayer.

Just as he raised his hand to knock, he heard voices from inside. Gabe's, raised in anger. Lisa's softer one, and another woman's voice.

Dara.

Dylan rapped on the door sharply, even as doubts crept into his thoughts. What was Dara doing here?

Footsteps sounded, approaching the door. It swung open and Lisa stood highlighted by the early-morning light coming through the living-room window. She wore loose pants and a T-shirt. Her hair framed her face in a tangled halo, but her eyes were hard. Even so, his heart skittered at the sight of her.

"What do you want?" she asked, both her hands holding the door like a shield. "I thought you had to leave today."

"My plane leaves in an hour. I have to talk to you."

"Dylan. What are you doing here?" Dara spun around, her cheeks flushed, her eyes bright. "I thought you were gone." In contrast to Lisa's casual wear, Dara wore a tailored suit, and even this early in the morning her hair was immaculately groomed.

"I've come to talk to Lisa and Gabe," Dylan said.

Gabe motioned for him to come in, netting him an irritated look from his sister-in-law. As Dylan walked past Lisa she glanced up at him, and for a heartbeat Dylan saw sorrow in the depths of her eyes. Then like a cloud sifting over the sun, it was gone. But it gave him hope.

"It's probably just as well you're here, Dylan," Dara said smoothly, suddenly in charge. She came to stand beside Dylan. "I've come on behalf of the company to tell Gabe that we are going to formally press charges of theft against him."

"You have no proof," Gabe exclaimed. "You know I didn't do it."

"Money in a numbered bank account put there by you." Dara shrugged, glancing at Dylan. "Dummy invoices signed by you for less than the actual amount. I can build a very strong case against you. And now that Dylan is here I know I finally have the support I need." Dara flashed him a bright smile. She touched him lightly, as if establishing a connection between them.

Dylan shook his head at Dara's obvious machinations, stepping away from her. Closer to Lisa. "Sorry, Dara. I'm not part of this. And we both know you don't really have a case."

"I have proof, Dylan," Dara said coldly.

"It won't stand up in a court of law," Dylan said. "And I won't let it get that far."

Lisa blinked then. Bit her lip and looked down.

Dylan took a chance and reached out to her. Cupped her shoulder with his hand. He felt the ragged edges of his day slowly becoming whole as she reached up and laid her hand over his. Maybe it was all going to work out after all.

"You are going to take these people's side against me?" Dara cried out. "Against us?"

Dylan, still holding Lisa's shoulder, turned to her. "Yes, Dara. If it comes to that I will." Dylan pushed down the lingering panic over his flight. The appointment, the future job didn't matter as much anymore. What was happening here was far more important.

"Your father will side with Ted and me. You know that. He always has. And where your father goes, your mother will."

"That doesn't matter," Dylan said quietly. "I believe Gabe didn't do it. And I'm going to support him and Lisa through whatever you decide to do."

"I guess we'll have to see about that," Dara snapped. "I'll be talking to your father next."

"Go ahead, Dara," Dylan said, holding her angry gaze. "You might be surprised to hear what he has to say."

He felt Lisa lean closer to him. Clutch his hand tighter. He turned to her, and as their eyes met Dylan was surprised to see the shimmer of tears in hers. He gave her a tentative smile, a small overture.

His entire attention was on Lisa as Dara stormed out of the apartment, slamming the door behind her.

"Thanks for coming," Lisa said softly. She sniffed, then wiped her eyes. Dylan touched one silvery tear as it slid down her cheek, wonderment and joy singing through him.

"I'm sorry I was so angry yesterday," he said softly, stroking her cheek with his knuckle.

"No. Please don't apologize. I'm the one who has to apologize. You were right. I had lied to you." Lisa palmed away some more tears. "I'm so sorry. I was going to tell you sometime. I felt so bad about deceiving you."

Gabe's discreet cough caught their attention. Suddenly self-conscious, Dylan lowered his hand.

"Sorry to break in on this very touching scene," Gabe said dryly, "but right now I'm sure Dara is heading right over to your parents' place, Dylan, or possibly even the police station."

"I don't think you need to worry about Dara," Dylan said. "She doesn't have the proof she thinks she does, nor the support."

Gabe frowned. "What do you mean?"

"My father had an inkling of what was going on. He won't allow her to pursue this."

"What are you saying?" Lisa asked, catching him by the arm.

"It's a long story. Why don't you and Gabe come with me to my parents' place? I'll fill you in on the way over."

"But you can't miss your flight," Lisa said. "You kept telling me how important that appointment was. For your future."

Dylan smiled at the concern in her voice. Concern for him. "Right now there are other parts of my future I'm more concerned with."

Lisa smiled as a faint flush crept up her cheeks. "But your job…"

"I think you had better be worrying about your own job." Dylan touched a finger to her lips, then caught her hand. "Now, enough arguing. Let's go."

But Lisa held back. "I don't need to come. Why don't you and Gabe go alone?"

"I want you along," Dylan said.

Lisa shook her head. "I can't, Dylan. I'm too ashamed."

Dylan glanced at Gabe. "Do you mind giving us a few moments?"

"I'll be waiting in the lobby." Gabe gave him a careful smile as if still unsure of how to read this new situation, and left the apartment.

Dylan waited until he heard Gabe's footsteps hitting the stairs, then turned back to Lisa. "You don't have to be afraid of my family," Dylan said softly, cupping her chin, pleased that he could.

"I'm more ashamed than anything. I lied to them about my brother," Lisa said, still not meeting his eyes. "And we both lied to them about us."

"Only in the beginning," Dylan said, stroking her cheek with his thumb. "The evening we had supper with my family, I wanted it to be real."

Lisa's faint smile gave him hope.

"Last night you told me that you'd found something you didn't want to let go. Is that still true?"

"Truer," she whispered, pressing her hand against his. "I love you."

A sharp fragment of happiness pierced his heart and his response was to draw her close. To tilt her head toward him and touch his lips gently to hers. "I love you, too," he whispered against her mouth.

She clung to him then, pressed her head against his chest as he held her close.

Dylan willed time to stand still. He felt as if he had waited all his life for this moment and he didn't want to return to everyday life.

"I thought you hated me," she said, her voice muffled against his shirt. "I didn't think I'd ever see you again."

Dylan stroked his chin over her head, marveling at his right to do so. To simply hold her close with no secrets between them anymore. "I missed you too much," he whispered, brushing a kiss across her temple. "I couldn't stay away."

"I'm sorry, Dylan."

"Stop now. You've done nothing worse than I have."

She drew back, a faint frown creasing her forehead. "Do you think God can bless a relationship that started out in deceit?"

Dylan smiled at her concern. "I think God used our situation to bring us to Him. I think if we put our trust in Him, put our lives in His hands, He will use us and our relationship to praise Him."

Lisa smiled. "You are a blessing to me, Dylan."

"And you to me, Lisa." He stroked her hair back from her face, dropped a light kiss on her forehead. "And I hate to bring reality into this moment, but your brother is waiting and I want to finish what we came here to do."

*   *   *

"Welcome to our home, Gabe." Stephanie held out her hand to Lisa's brother. "Alex is waiting for you on the deck." Gabe shook Stephanie's hand, then glanced at Lisa, as if for support.

His unconscious gesture made Lisa's heart contract with old memories of meetings with other authorities when Gabe had gotten into trouble. How he always looked to her for help.

And she'd always been there. Just as she was now. She was about to reassure him.

"It's okay, Gabe," Dylan said suddenly. "We're here to sort things out."

Gabe nodded, smoothed his hair back from his face and walked out the large glass doors. As they slid shut behind him, Lisa glanced at Dylan, pleased at his support. And then it struck her with a wave of pleasure. She wasn't doing this alone anymore.

"Dylan, darling, I hate to point out the obvious, but didn't you and Lisa have a plane to catch?" Stephanie glanced over her shoulder. "In about twenty minutes?"

"I did, Mother. But Lisa and I didn't have a proper chance to say goodbye."

Stephanie angled him a puzzled glance. "But if you do that you'll miss…" She raised her hands in a gesture of defeat. "Can you please tell me what's going on?"

"Dylan," Lisa said softly. "I want to tell her."

Dylan nodded, took her hand and squeezed it lightly.

"Sorry, Mom," he said with a smile. " Why don't

you sit down? Lisa and I have something to tell you.''

Stephanie's eyes grew wide and her mouth slipped open as she looked from Dylan to Lisa.

Help me through this, Lord, Lisa prayed. *I want her respect as much as I crave Dylan's.*

And slowly, hesitatingly, Lisa told Stephanie all about her deception.

''I want to say I'm sorry, Stephanie,'' Lisa said, her voice urgent. ''I know I was wrong. I deceived you and Alex and the girls.''

''You're forgiven, if that's what you need to hear,'' Stephanie said with a smile.

''Just like that?''

''Of course, my dear.'' Stephanie drew Lisa into her arms and held her close. Just as a mother would. ''Just like that. I can't withhold my forgiveness from you when God has forgiven me so much more.''

And once again Lisa felt hot tears prick her eyelids.

The chimes of the doorbell echoed through the house.

''I suspect that's Ted and Dara,'' Dylan said with a tired sigh.

Lisa's heartbeat kicked up a notch at the thought of confronting Dara again. She glanced over her shoulder through the glass doors to where Alex and Gabe sat in earnest conversation. She prayed it would all work out.

''How can you take the word of someone who lied to you all?'' Dara said, her face flushed with emotion. She sat ramrod straight in her chair, her eyes flashing, her very posture displaying the tension in her voice. Beside her, Ted leaned back in his chair, his lips pressed in a thin line, his eyes narrowed.

Dara's eyes flicked from Alex to Stephanie but avoided Dylan, Lisa and Gabe. It was as if they didn't even exist for her.

"Gabe lied about his involvement with the police," Dara continued, stating her case in a cold, clear voice. "Lisa lied about her involvement with Gabe." She raised her hands in a dramatic gesture. "I don't know about you, but to me that makes much of what they say suspect."

Dylan ignored his anger at Dara's accusations. Instead he glanced sidelong at Lisa. Her cheeks were red, but her head was unbowed. He covered her hand with his under the table and gave it a reassuring squeeze.

"I think you should be careful who you condemn, Dara," Alex said, leaning forward. He folded his hands on the table and held Dara's gaze. "What I'd like to know more about is your personal knowledge about the missing money."

"Wait a minute." Dara's mouth fell open in shock. "I'm not the one that took it...." She gestured toward Gabe. "Ask him. He knows."

"Dara, do you know why I asked Dylan to come here, against your will?" Alex asked, his voice quiet, his gaze direct.

"No."

"I was hoping that his coming here would send a signal to you and to Ted. A signal that I had my doubts about Gabe's guilt.'' He picked up the file folder in front of him and tapped it lightly on the table. ''I was hoping that you would come forward and tell me what I wanted to hear without us having to involve outside people. And now, in spite of your lack of cooperation and in spite of limited material available to Dylan and Lisa, they still managed to find some pieces of information that don't look good for you.''

Dara drooped back against her chair and for a moment Dylan felt sorry for her. Though Alex had given her and Ted the opportunity to talk to him in private, she had opted for this public moment. And this was the result.

''How do you... How can you...'' She faltered, reaching out for Ted. ''Ted, help me.''

Ted took his wife's hand between his. ''What information did you find, Dad?''

''Lisa told Dylan about the time on the bank deposit. It happened after Gabe left the office.''

Dara glared at Lisa as if making one last-ditch effort. ''Whatever it was you did to Gabe's computer, that can be found out. You must have jimmied the files yourself.''

''Be careful what you say, Dara,'' Dylan said, a warning tone edging his voice.

''Is that all you have, Dad?'' Ted asked, rubbing his index finger over his eyebrow.

Alex glanced at Dylan, who nodded, then he pushed the file folder across the table.

Ted opened it, glanced over the memo, then back at Dara. He said nothing. Just showed it to her. Dara glanced at the memo, blanched visibly and shook her head. "This can't be right. This…this is a fake."

"Dara, stop this now," Ted said softly. "I want to help you. I don't want this to get worse."

Dara looked down. Shook her head. "Why are you doing this, Ted?"

"Because I care about you."

And in that moment Dylan felt a grudging respect for Ted. And saw that the legacy of faithful love had been passed on from the father to his children.

Dara ran one carefully manicured fingernail over a faint gouge in the table. "All you care about is the company. Showing your father that you're as good a man as Dylan is."

Ted gave his brother a vague smile. "I'm not."

Dara pressed her nail deeper. "Then why were you always gone? Why were all our conversations about the company and how you were supposed to try to run it? Why did you stop paying attention to me?"

And Dylan got an inkling of why Dara had done what she had.

"Well, you got my attention these past few days."

"I don't want it just for a few days." Dara spun around, tears gathering in her perfectly made up eyes. "I want you to be a part of my life all the time. And it just wasn't happening." The tears slipped down her cheeks, and with a jerky movement she got up from her chair and left.

Ted got up and carefully pushed both their chairs back under the table. "Sorry about this, Dad. Mom." He gave Dylan an apologetic look. "I was wrong,

Dylan. I really thought she was telling me the truth. I'm sorry for what she said to you and how she spoke about Lisa.''

Dylan felt a rush of love for his brother at the admission that he knew was difficult to make. "We'll talk later. I think Dara needs you now.''

"I guess I never realized she always did." And then he left.

The hollow drip of the kitchen tap echoed in the heavy silence that followed.

Stephanie cleared her throat and looked around. "I think we should pray for them," she said softly.

She held out her hand to Lisa on one side, Alex on the other. Dylan took Lisa's hand and squeezed it lightly. She responded as they bowed their heads. But Alex was the one who prayed.

The moment of silence that followed his father's quietly spoken prayer was a moment of communion Dylan hadn't felt in a long time. As he looked up, he caught his father's eye.

And for the first time in many years he felt a deep and abiding respect for his father.

Stephanie got up from the table, looking around. "Well, I did have a special breakfast made for Dylan, who ran out before he could have any. It's still ready if anyone wants it.''

Dylan couldn't help but laugh. Food. His mother's cure-all. "What do you have for me, Mom?''

"Your favorite. Crepes with strawberries and whipped cream and fruit," Stephanie said wistfully.

"Well, heat them up now. I'm sure Lisa and Gabe would love to try them.''

With a pleased smile Stephanie got up and started working in the kitchen, declining Lisa's offer of help.

While she worked, Dylan turned to his father. Smiled. "I have an apology to make to you, Dad."

Alex held up his hand. "I understand, Dylan. It's okay."

"But I still need to tell you that I'm sorry. For doubting you. For being so angry at how you handled this very delicate situation."

Alex shook his head. "No. I'm sorry. I should have told you right from the beginning." He lifted one shoulder in a shrug. "I was too proud. I guess I was hoping I could solve the problem without you knowing how badly I had failed the company."

"I can understand that," Dylan said. "I guess pride is something we both share." He glanced sidelong at Lisa, who was watching this exchange with a wistful smile tugging at her lips. He took her hand and gave it a light shake. "And what is going on behind those beautiful brown eyes?"

"This family." Lisa shook her head in amazement. "You apologize in front of complete strangers. You are willing to admit your faults. You are a gift to each other."

"Amen to that," Alex said.

Dylan felt a rush of love, strong and pure. He wished he and Lisa could be alone, could talk. Take the time to right the wrongs of the past few days. Reconnect as Christians.

Breakfast was over. The dishes were done, but everyone lingered around the table.

Alex was talking to Gabe. "Things are still a little up in the air with the company, Gabe, but I'm fairly sure once we get the books properly audited by a disinterested third party, the full truth will come to light. I was wondering if you would want your job back."

Lisa's fingers dug into Dylan's hand, her eyes now on Gabe.

Gabe pursed his lips, considering. "Actually, I would prefer if I could get a reference from your company. There are a few other places I think I might like to work for instead."

"I understand," Alex said softly. "And once again, I'm so sorry for what you've had to go through. You're very lucky to have a sister who is willing to take risks for you."

"I sure am," Gabe said, his smile gentle. "She always says family takes care of family."

Dylan waited a beat. Allowed the moment to settle.

"Lisa. We need to talk," he said, squeezing her hand.

Without looking at him, she nodded, as if suddenly shy.

"Mom. Dad. Gabe. I hope you'll excuse us a moment," Dylan said, looking around the group.

"You're not going to try to catch your flight?"

Dylan laughed as he stood, drawing Lisa to her feet. "I think I've given up on that completely." He glanced at his father. Smiled. "I might have a few other plans to discuss with my father."

"I'll be waiting," Alex said.

Dylan slipped his arm around Lisa and gave her a quick one-armed hug. "Let's go," he said softly.

She looked up at him, a coy smile playing around her lips. "You're not my boss anymore, you know."

"I know. And I'm going to miss having the authority." He gave her hand a tug. "C'mon. Let's go for a walk."

Lisa wrapped her sweater a little closer. "Speaking as a former employee, I think missing your flight's not going to create the best impression." The damp path they were walking along meandered through dense undergrowth shadowed by tall fir trees, which created a microclimate both cool and secluded. "West Coast rainforest," the plaque along the path had said. Lisa was thankful she had worn the sweater Dylan had recommended she take along.

They had been walking for quite a while now. Lisa was surprised at the size of this park, a serene and secluded place bracketed by development on three sides.

"It is awkward," Dylan agreed. He sauntered along beside her, his hands in the pockets of his blue jeans, looking unconcerned about her pronouncement. "I'm not so sure I want the job after all."

"Perry Hatcher is taking over your position in Toronto." Lisa felt silly pointing out the obvious, but felt as if she was carefully navigating territory as unfamiliar to her as the path they were walking down.

"And I suspect he'll have to look for another secretary," Dylan said casually.

Lisa only nodded, unsure what to say.

I know I don't deserve anything, Lord, Lisa prayed as they walked on in silence. *But I do want to make things right between us. At least that.*

They met another couple holding hands and as Dylan and Lisa stepped aside to let them by, Lisa noticed that the woman was pregnant. The couple thanked them and walked on, caught up in their conversation.

Lisa's eyes followed them.

"You've done that before," Dylan said softly, coming to a halt beside the path.

"What do you mean?" Lisa stopped beside him, uncertain what he was talking about.

"I remember when we first arrived in Vancouver, we were driving through Stanley Park. You saw a couple pushing a baby buggy. You did the same thing you just did now. Watched them like it was something wonderful."

"It is, I guess—wonderful, that is. Wonderful to see a family together like that. People happy to be together."

"Are you happy to be with me?"

Lisa's gaze flew to his, the wistful note in his voice catching her attention.

"Yes. I am."

"Do you like Vancouver?"

"I love it. It's a beautiful city."

"I like it, too. It's home." Dylan's smile held a tinge of melancholy. "In spite of how crazy things have been this past week, I was glad to be back here."

"I enjoyed *most* of our visit here."

"Which part did you like the best?"

Lisa smiled, took a chance and laid her hands on his chest. "Sailing with you. Being alone with you with no one around. It was the first time we were together and we weren't pretending."

Dylan laid his hands over hers, warming them. "I wasn't pretending very often," he said softly.

Lisa held his gaze. Saw the sincerity in it and made her own confession.

"Neither was I."

And suddenly she was in his arms. Held close to him. Being kissed by him. She returned his kiss as joy surged through her.

"I know this is crazy," he murmured, holding her close, stroking her hair with his hand. "But I feel like I've known you for years. I feel like we belong together."

In spite of the joy his words gave her, she couldn't stop the whisper of guilt and doubt that circled. "I wish I had told you everything at the beginning," she started. "But I couldn't…"

Dylan stopped her words with his mouth, then drew back, touching her face. "We talked about this already. We have forgiven each other. I know God has forgiven us. This is a beginning of its own, Lisa. A beginning of something better than what came before. I want to spend the rest of my life with you. I don't care where that happens or how, but I just know that since I met you, I don't want to be away from you. I want to give you all the things you haven't been able to have. I want to share my family with you, my life. Everything I have.''

Lisa felt her throat grow thick with tears of happiness. ''I'm going to cry again,'' she warned, her lips trembling.

''That's okay. I'm patient.''

''Love is patient,'' she whispered. ''I wish I could tell you what a blessing you've been to me.''

''And you for me.''

And as he kissed her again, Lisa felt that this truly was the beginning.

Epilogue

"**W**here should I put the balloons?" Amber yanked on the string of helium balloons, making them bounce in the open space of the foyer.

"Give those to me. I'll tie them along the banister," Stephanie suggested.

"Erika has a bunch, too."

"My goodness, you girls. How did you get them all in your car?"

"We borrowed Gabe's," Amber said with a grin.

"You girls better stop taking advantage of him." Stephanie tut-tutted. "He just got that car."

"He wanted to come along."

"I'm glad he could take time off. They work him too hard at that job of his," Stephanie said. "Anyhow, I want you to help Chelsea in the kitchen. She's getting the food ready. And hurry."

The door opened, and Stephanie jumped. But it was only Alex and Erika dwarfed by a batch of balloons even bigger than the one Amber was carrying. Gabe was with her.

"You guys scared me," Stephanie said, her hand on her heart. "I thought you were Dylan and Lisa."

Alex grinned at her and gave her a quick kiss. "I stopped by the office before I came here. Dylan had some work to do yet, and then he was going to pick up Lisa on his way here."

"Too bad Ted and Dara couldn't be here, too."

Alex nodded. "Toronto is a bit far to come just for this."

"Bring those to the kitchen," Stephanie said to Gabe and Erika. "Chelsea, Jordan and Amber can figure out what to do with them." She turned back to Alex. "Anything interesting come in the mail?"

He nodded and held up a letter. "This from Ted and Dara."

Stephanie snatched it out of his hands, her eyes skimming hungrily over the cramped writing. She looked up at Alex. "What do you think? Do they sound happy?"

"I think having him work at the Toronto branch was a move in the right direction," Alex said, dropping a light kiss on his wife's forehead. "And now you better hurry. Dylan and Lisa are only minutes behind me."

The kitchen was a flurry of activity, but minutes later all was in order.

"They're coming," Erika called out from her vantage point at the top of the stairs. "Get ready." She sped down the stairs, sending the balloons swaying in her wake.

Giggles were suppressed as they heard Dylan's and Lisa's muffled voices.

Then the door opened and everyone jumped out.

"Surprise."

"Happy anniversary."

The shouts blended into a cacophony of sound and celebration.

Dylan and Lisa stood in the doorway, their mouths open. And then they were hugged and kissed and congratulated again.

"You guys. I was wondering what was going on," Lisa said, grinning as she looked around the room.

Dylan just shook his head.

"Kiss her, Dylan!" Amber shouted.

"Oh, like he never does," Chelsea said. "C'mon. Let's eat. I'm starved."

They moved en masse to the kitchen. When the noise and busyness had died down and they were all settled at the table, food in front of them, Alex stood up.

"I just want to say an official congratulations to Dylan and Lisa," he said, smiling at the happy couple who sat at the opposite end of the table. Dylan had his arm slung over Lisa's shoulder and she was leaning into him, her cheeks flushed and her eyes sparkling as she looked around the table full of people. "I want to say how much we've enjoyed watching our newest daughter and our son grow closer together in their first year of marriage. And closer to God. I want to thank God for His blessing on our family. For His love. A love that, like Dylan and

Lisa's wedding text said, is never ending but most of all patient.''

And as his father spoke, a smile broke across Dylan's face. Then he turned to his wife and kissed her, their love for each other shining in their eyes.

* * * * *

Dear Reader,

Family is the place where we can experience both our deepest hurts and our deepest love. What I was hoping to show in *Love Is Patient* is that even in the "best" families, mistakes are made, sometimes with the best intentions. Though our children are all adults by the world's standards, we are still involved in their lives and make mistakes in them.

I'm always thankful that we have a perfect Father in God and that His love for us doesn't depend on our behaviors.

PS: I love to hear from my readers. You can write to me at:

Carolyne Aarsen,
Box 114,
Neerlandia, AB,
T0G 1R0
Canada.

Carolyne Aarsen